AF497774

MURDER AT THE WEDDING

NADISHKA ALOYSIUS

CHAPTER ONE

HELP! SOMEONE HAS murdered the Bard!"

I looked up with a start and swung my legs off my bed at the sound of my best friend Vino's voice echoing from the sitting room outside. Then, the door to my bedroom slammed open and Vino herself stood in the doorway, waving a sheet of glossy paper.

"What?" I asked, confused. "Who killed the Bard? Hasn't he been dead for four hundred years?"

It was Vino's turn to look confused. "Bard? Who said anything about Shakespeare?"

I snapped my book shut. I hate having to put down a good murder mystery just before the denouement, but this piqued my natural curiosity.

"You did. Just now," I pointed out. "You hollered for the whole of Parkaduwa to hear that someone had murdered the Bard."

Vino flung herself into the only chair in the room. "No Kiyama. I said, 'Someone has murdered the *Bride*.' Not Bard."

She must have noticed the bewilderment on my face because she launched into a lengthy explanation. "It's this brochure. It came in the post. The Falcon's Rest Hotel is hosting a murder mystery dinner and the theme is a Sri Lankan wedding. It's twenty-five thousand rupees per head for the entire experience, lodging and meals. I thought it would be fun to attend."

I grinned. This was so typical of Vino. She was always hankering after something new. "But it wouldn't be much of a mystery if we know in advance who's going to die."

Vino flapped the brochure in my direction. "*No,*" she said, elongating the vowel and rolling her eyes. "Of course we don't. That was just me voicing my excitement!"

I held out my hand with a sigh. "Let me see if I can untangle this."

It was a standard triple fold brochure printed full colour on art paper. One side boasted the many amenities of the hotel while the other advertised the event: MURDER MOST FOWL.

I burst out laughing. "It looks more like a murder mystery in a chicken coop! Or maybe we need to capture our own bird for the feast!" Tears filled my eyes as I giggled uncontrollably.

Vino reached out and plucked the paper from my unprotesting fingers. "Not everyone has a background in English literature," she said with a mock frown. But then she chuckled. "I didn't even notice that typo! I just skipped to the part about the wedding. It's here on the next page."

She cleared her throat and read aloud:

> **"Calling all murder mystery enthusiasts – can you solve this one?**
> **Enjoy the experience of a lifetime**
> **Spend a night at the Falcon's Rest Hotel and pit your wits against a cunning murderer**
> **All guests will be assigned a role**
> **The theme for the event is a Sri Lankan poruwa wedding.**
> **Rs 25 000 per person (food and lodging included)**
> **Only 13 spots so book your place ASAP**
> **Call ...**

And there is a local number," she finished.

"Let me get this straight," I said. "They're organizing a fake wedding… with *thirteen* guests… and someone pretends to get murdered… and the guests have to solve the crime?"

"In a nutshell, yes. I think that's how it works."

"Isn't that asking for trouble?"

Vino grinned. "Not everyone finds a body in a paddy field and solves the case before the cops. That's our specialty. Besides, what are the chances of the same thing happening again? Like they say, lightning doesn't strike twice."

"Oh, please, do not remind me of that incident. I'd rather not have to hunt for clues, interview suspects and face down a gun-toting sociopath again! Once in a lifetime is more than enough, thank you!"

I shifted on my bed as silence descended. I could see from the faraway look in Vino's eyes that she too was recalling 'The Incident'. Three months back, when I first moved to Vino's bungalow at Parkaduwa, we were dragged into a murder investigation before I had even unpacked my luggage. A local teacher named Priyanka was found in a paddy field and the cops immediately homed in on Vino's relationship with him. That prompted us to run a counter investigation to clear her name. I shuddered as I recalled that final climatic night. The bumps and bruises had disappeared in a few days, but the nightmares had lasted a lot longer.

"I'm just beginning to sleep well through the night," I said. "I don't want to relive that affair!"

"Me neither." Vino's voice was solemn, and she looked me in the eye. "But I think this would be a great way to finally bury the past, don't you think?"

I sighed. She had a point. Since 'The Incident' life had continued at a sedate pace. My resolution to take a break from my marriage still held and I had not returned to Colombo despite numerous text messages from my husband, Andy. Vino and I had quickly fallen into a routine. Hopefully, participating in a staged murder mystery would change the status quo; life in rural Sri Lanka was a little dull.

"Alright," I agreed. "Let's do this. I think we're both getting far too stiff and staid and although Parkaduwa is growing on me I don't want to stagnate here. A little fun and excitement, and a few new faces should be a welcome change…" I caught the gleam in Vino's eye and added, "And, no, I am not looking for a new man in my life, Vino, so don't get started!"

Two weeks flew by, and it was soon time to pack a bag and get ourselves to the hotel.

> *"Kick up a rumpus*
> *But don't lose the compass*
> *And get me to the church on time!"*

I stopped singing as Vino appeared at the doorway. "It should be 'Get me to the poruwa', you know!"

"I guess I'm feeling kind of impatient about the whole thing, now that I've had to endure a two week wait. And, no," I continued before Vino could interrupt, "I do not want to get *me* to the church, poruwa or anywhere else anytime soon!"

"Oh, come on Kiy!" said Vino, in mock exasperation. "*I'm* not getting married anytime soon, and you can't blame a girl for trying. Matchmaking is fun!"

"Yeah, you may just let Bridezilla loose!" I retorted.

"That's a bet. If you get the role of the bride today, I'll pay your event ticket money, I want you to be a real *Bridezilla* for the duration of the event!"

I laughed. "You're on! But it works both ways, you know. If you get to be the bride then *you* have to be the Bridezilla, deal?"

We shook on it.

Vino peered into my bag. "Are you ready? Have you packed your saree?"

I gaped at her for a second before it dawned on me that she was pulling my leg. I punched her lightly on the arm. "Not funny, Vino! You know how I feel about six yards of cloth…"

"You'd rather be enclosed in a shroud. Yes, I recall the little tantrum I had to endure while dressing you up as a respectable government teacher!"

I hid a grin. I had not realized I missed this friendly banter until I re-established my friendship with Vino. I placed my hands on my hips and struck the most theatrical pose I could. "Tantrum? Huh! Let's see *your* saree then?"

She was laughing so hard she could barely speak. She waved a hand in front of her. "Okay, okay. Guilty as charged. I didn't pack a saree either. You know something, it's going to be a weird poruwa ceremony without the trappings. But that's not our problem."

She got up. "Shall we?"

I hefted my bag. "Yes, we shall."

Vino and I chose to forego our usual means of transport – bicycles – and I drove my yellow Maruti the short distance to The Falcon's Rest instead. It felt good to take her out after a long break, although it took us twice as long to get to our destination, and I winced at every bone-wrenching jolt.

"Why don't the residents just pool in and fix this road?" I complained, as I almost hit my head on the inner ceiling of the vehicle.

"Because it is not a private road. It's supposed to be maintained by the government. And the general view is that since we pay taxes, we should not also have to pay to fix the road. Believe me, I tried as soon as I moved here. No one else was interested. In fact, I heard some mutterings about 'new-fangled notions from Colombo' so I kept my mouth shut after that."

I winced again as the undercarriage grazed an exceptionally large rock in the centre of the road. Living in the countryside had its ups and downs, literally. "Well, I guess bouncing around once a month is not too bad," I said, referring to our monthly run to Ratnapura for supplies. "Which reminds me, we need to get more muesli next time."

I navigated my way around craters that would have put the moon to shame and finally reached the main road. Main Street of Parkaduwa town was nothing much – just a few shops lining either side of the B5 road that ran through to Eheliya town ten kilometres away. I drove past the bus depot, Saradha Stores (a small grocery shop), Harini Textiles, and Richy Bakers. Soon the Parkaduwa Central College loomed rigid on our right. I smiled as I recalled my disastrous two-day stint there as a substitute teacher. That had driven home the fact that teaching English language at a government school was definitely not for me. It had also prompted me to rethink my career options. I am a qualified English literature teacher. Since there is no demand for that here, I accepted Vino's offer to undertake some of her secretarial work from home. She was unable to hire someone with sufficient language skills to correspond with buyers overseas and I needed a job, so it has worked out. For now.

I rested the engine at the top of a rise and surveyed the road which sloped downwards leading out of town. The infamous 'body in the paddy field' was discovered not far from this spot. I remembered clearly how Vino and I had been on a cycle tour of the town that day and observed the discovery first-hand. The lack of multi-storey buildings made this a good vantage point to take in the surrounding fields which resembled a patchwork quilt of emerald-green, white, and brown. Towering over the paddy fields was a large, white, old-fashioned building – the Falcon's Rest Hotel.

I sped down and veered off into a path on my right which was marked by a massive billboard announcing the presence of the hotel to the world. Personally, I am not a fan of spoiling the rural beauty of the area with monstrous cut-outs, but the residents had not objected, so here it was. It did make the hotel so much easier to find. And since the hotel was now the biggest employer in town, it was in everyone's best interest that potential customers did not find themselves wandering aimlessly among the paddy fields.

Imposing pillars and an ornate iron gate marked the entrance while a long driveway lined by a beautifully maintained garden led up to the building. It was easy to overlook the poverty of the local farmers when faced with a structure such as this. My thoughts flew back to our first visit here. The building had then been partially renovated. The large fountain at the entrance had been dry. The garden paths had barely been paved. There had been a skeleton staff.

Vino and I had not visited the hotel since 'The Incident' and I smiled as I surveyed the building. We had made no effort to meet the new owner, but small-town gossip being what it was, we were up to date on the latest news. Examining the fully renovated premises I realized he had worked fast to prepare the place for the tourist season. And the Murder Most Fowl event must be his first attempt at attracting a crowd.

A porter ran up and collected our bags as soon as we alighted from the vehicle.

"Please, please, walk right in, Miss Kiyama. I can handle this! How are you doing, Miss Vino?" he exclaimed with an exaggerated bow and a smile.

I did a double take as I noted the figure in the ill-fitting white shirt. "Siril?"

The short, thin man's grin grew wider. "Yes, Miss! I'm so honoured you remember me! Amma got me this job and so far, it has been good. Please, don't stay out here burning in the hot sun. Go in. Go in!"

Vino and I exchanged amused glances as we walked up to the main door. Siril was our cook Manike's son whom we had used as a guide during our last adventure. To be honest, he had not been helpful or resourceful, really, and had bolted like a frightened rabbit at the first hint of trouble.

"He didn't strike me as a particularly industrious fellow, when he slunk away and abandoned us to Inspector de Silva. I hope he sticks to the job here," Vino commented, reading my mind.

I envisioned our vociferous cook in full flow. "Yes, Manike will have a lot to say if he gets fired. Or if he leaves saying it's too strenuous or tedious."

Vino shrugged. "We'll hear about it from her, either way!"

The carved front doors stood open. A doorman in a smart uniform greeted us with the traditional gesture of placing both palms together. "Ayubowan! Good Afternoon!"

"Good Afternoon!" we replied as we walked in.

"May I help you, Madam?"

"Yes, please. We're here for the Murder Mystery Event."

"Please follow me," he said as he escorted us to the reception desk.

I gazed around as I strolled in. The colour scheme and décor were as I recalled - bright and welcoming. The fittings and furniture in the lobby had not changed either. The new owner had obviously decided to cut costs and leave the completed areas as they were. The infamous plush armchairs where we had faced down our adversary were still present but placed in a different corner of the room. I shuddered inwardly and decided I would not be relaxing in those chairs anytime soon.

The reception counter had not been installed when I visited three months ago. Behind the ornately carved polished wood was a young girl also dressed in a colourful handloom uniform. The entrance hall was wall-to-wall with luggage, and helpers wound their way through the maze. The receptionist looked overworked so I informed the doorman that we would take a stroll and return later to check in.

We made our way down the long corridor that led to the pool and back garden. Vino squeezed my hand as we stepped out. Memories flooded in but I wasn't overcome by nausea or dizziness as I walked by the pool and past the changing rooms without a fault in my steps. Congratulating myself for finally laying the demons to rest, I whispered, "How are you feeling?"

She cleared her throat and said, "I think being here in broad daylight helps. And I think we need to get into the pool as soon as possible and wash away the memories, you know?"

"That's a great idea. Let's order some cocktails as well and relax until the event starts."

I noticed Siril running up to us.

"Miss Vino. Miss Kiyama. The receptionist asked me to tell you the crowd has lessened, and you can check in at your leisure," he announced, each of the last three words accompanied by an emphatic nod.

I raised an eyebrow at Vino. Although Siril reminded me of a wound up Noddy toy, he also sounded impressively polished and professional, and I wondered if the new owner had brought in a trainer from Colombo to give the new staff an introduction into the hospitality industry.

We followed our enthusiastic guide to the lobby, which was now, thankfully, empty.

"Kiyama Fernando and Vinodhini Dias," I informed the receptionist, "We called about two weeks ago and made a booking for today's event?"

"Yes, Miss," she replied as she noted our details, accepted payment, and handed us an old-fashioned key. "You will be in Room 204."

"No automated key cards?" I asked with a smile as I tucked it into my handbag.

"No," she answered. "Mr. Peiris, the owner, felt that would upset the atmosphere of the place."

"And I agree," Vino joined in. "This place is charming! By the way, how many have signed up for the Mystery Event?"

"We have a full house for that, Miss. All our guests are participating," the girl replied.

"A full house! Mr. Peiris must be ecstatic!"

"Yes," she acknowledged, "the details are in this docket. There is a guest list and the schedule for the events. The introduction will be this evening at 6 p.m. at the Rooftop Lounge."

"Thank you so much, Shanti," I said, reading her name tag.

Siril was bouncing on his toes by our side, our bags in hand. "I'll show you the way, Miss. Come this way!"

I inhaled deeply as I stepped into the lift.

Our weekend getaway steeped in murder and mystery was about to begin.

CHAPTER TWO

ROOM 204 WAS at the end of a carpeted corridor. The bright Sri Lankan theme continued on the second floor with local artwork and sculptures placed strategically throughout the open area. Siril opened the door dramatically and bowed us into a large room with one king size bed, an elegant couch, and carved closets. The floor was made of wood and French windows opened out to a small balcony.

"Nice," I breathed as I looked around. "Please leave our bags here, Siril."

He beamed as I slipped a few notes into his hand. "Ask for me any time of the day, Miss, if you need anything at all. If you want extra pillows, things carried down to the pool, room service… anything!" he said as he bowed out.

Vino and I both laughed as soon as the door shut behind him.

"What have they done to the ferrety little guy who left us high and dry at Ariyawansa's place a few months ago?" Vino asked.

"Whoever trained the staff should receive an award!" I commented.

Vino sat on the bed and bounced a few times. She patted the large fluffy pillows and smoothed the duvet. "Very nice."

The room was decorated in shades of blue. A large modern art mural adorned the wall behind the bed. A smaller one of similar design was on the wall opposite. A large flat screen television took pride of place on the desk. The lights were dimmed. I walked to the large window and drew back the heavy curtains. The small balcony featuring a rattan sofa overlooked the beautiful paddy fields that stretched across the horizon. The swimming pool below was a rectangle of sparkling blue just below us.

No traffic. No concrete jungle. I breathed in deeply savouring the crisp, fresh air.

The bed was an old-fashioned four-poster, but with white mosquito nets rather than bed curtains. It was rather high off the floor. Vino had no problem with this. She swung her long lanky frame up on to the bed and stretched out. I, however, grimaced. I would have to hop in and out.

"Oh, dignity be damned!" I muttered as I grabbed the dossier we received at the reception and lifted myself onto the bed and lay down.

Vino had closed her eyes.

"Hey," I nudged her. "Don't doze off! We're going down to the pool, remember? And it looks like there's plenty of shelf space in those cupboards so we might as well unpack. No need to live out of a backpack here."

I flipped idly through the pages, commenting as I went. "So, the receptionist said the hotel is full, and she mentioned there's a guest list in here somewhere." I rummaged through the papers. "Ah, here it is. Let's see… Our names are right at the top. We must have booked the first two tickets! Then there's a Tracy and Harold Malwatte, they must be a married couple. I bet they're in their sixties at least with names like that! There are three females next, maybe they came in a group? Serena Perera, Minosha Wijewardene and Kumudu Kariyawasam. Hamzah and Riaz Fariz, they must be married as well. Chris David. Chamil Hewage. Megan Stewart. Robert Vermak."

I glanced at Vino who was listening in interest.

"A bit difficult to guess their backgrounds. Some of the names are fairly generic. I mean, Chris David could be a Sri Lankan or a foreigner."

"The last two are definitely foreigners. Could be visiting or expats?"

"Yes," I agreed. "It's highly unlikely that Megan Stewart and Robert Vermak are locals!"

"Harold Malwatte sounds familiar… I wonder if I met him while working in Colombo," said Vino.

"Darling! This is Sri Lanka! You are bound to know somebody's somebody! Wait and see. That will be the first thing established this evening!"

Vino laughed. "Yes, true. It's a very Sri Lankan thing, isn't it? The moment we meet someone we try to figure out if they are connected to us in any way."

"Six degrees of separation."

"A lot less than that!" Vino consulted her wristwatch. "We have some time. There's no point going down to the pool until after four o'clock. Let's play a game."

I raised an eyebrow.

"Let's try to guess everyone's profession and maybe some background as well."

"Fantastic!" I grinned and read the list. "Let's start with the Malwattes. I think he's a doctor. And she doesn't work. Probably a society lady of Colombo."

Vino shook her head in mock despair. "Just because someone doesn't work doesn't mean she's living in high style!" She inclined her head at me. "Case in point?"

I swatted a pillow at her. "I work! Part time. For you!"

"Okay, my turn," said Vino as she took the list. "Serena Perera… She sounds like a fashion designer or some other artsy type."

I shrugged. "Could be. Who's next? Minosha Wijewardene. That's a tough one. I can't picture anything for that name."

"Minosha… Minosha…" Vino repeated the name as if trying to taste it on her tongue. "I think she's a student of some form or the other."

"Okay, let's go with that for now," I agreed. "Kumudu Kariyawasam… That's a nice alliterative name."

"Only a teacher of English literature would notice that!"

"Well, it is! Anyway, I think she's a teacher," I retorted.

"Or a scientist or inventor," suggested Vino.

I looked at her in surprise. "What gave you that idea?"

"Just a feeling."

I shrugged. "Okay. Next one. Hamzah and Riaz Fariz. I don't want to be discriminatory, but a lot of Muslims are business owners."

"I'll go with that."

"Now to the intriguing lot," I said. "Chris David."

"Airline pilot or steward," said Vino immediately.

I gaped at her. "Where did that come from?"

"I don't know. Just popped into my head. I'm also trying to think up more professions. We've covered teacher, doctor, businessman, designer and student so far."

I laughed. "That's a weird way of doing it! There could be more than one of each profession! We may have two doctors or two lawyers… Wait a second. We didn't assign lawyer to anyone and there's always one of those lurking around. So, I think Chamil Hewage is a lawyer."

Vino chuckled. "This is a lot more fun than I anticipated. We have only the two foreigners left, right? They can go as tourists, for now."

"Done," I said, turning the page. "Let's see what they've planned for us and how this event is going to work."

There were two sealed envelopes marked PRIVATE AND CONFIDENTIAL hidden between the pages. One had my name on the cover and the other was addressed to Vinodhini Dias. Under our names was a handwritten message

Do not share with your roommate.

Secrecy is crucial to the success of the event

She hugged the envelope to her chest and made a shooing motion with her hand. "Don't peek! I may be the detective and you may be the murderer!"

I rolled my eyes and moved to the foot of the bed, while she sat up at the other end. Together we tore open our envelopes.

"This is a comprehensive guide to what we should and should not do," I said, reading off the paper. "There's also a card with our character traits. I guess we can carry that around with us to consult during the event. I'm the Mother of the Groom. Who are you?"

"I'm sworn to secrecy!" she said in a dramatic whisper.

I kicked her lightly. "Oh, just tell me your character!"

"I'm a Bridesmaid."

"Did you read through the instructions? It says there is no set script, and we have to improvise. We need to mingle and extract information from the other participants, while revealing certain facts about ourselves. There will be clues hidden around the room, like in a scavenger hunt and we need to collect as many as we can and guess the killer."

I paused to consider this. "Sounds straight forward."

"You missed the part about selecting a name," interrupted Vino. "There's a card with a lanyard and we have to write our name for the event. Isn't that going to be confusing? We will have to introduce ourselves with our real names before the event and then remember to answer to our character names later on!"

"And, it says there will be prizes for the participants. That's nice! I hope I get a box of chocolates." I firmly believed that a girl can never have too much chocolate. Was it any wonder that J. K. Rowling prescribed chocolate as medication for encounters with dementors?

Vino tossed a pillow at me. "What happened to your diet?"

"I'm on a cheat day," I replied without missing a beat.

She held her hands up. "Hey, I have nothing against eating well, as long as you're healthy! You're the one who's always moaning about putting on weight!"

I groaned. "Please, don't remind me! I have to wear a swimsuit in front of the rest of the hotel guests in about an hour! Speaking of which, we'd better unpack and get ready to head down."

I swung my legs off the bed and looked around the room. The furniture looked antique and elegant. I am not a connoisseur, but I detest cheap, fibreboard furniture so it was a pleasure to relax in such comfort.

"Oh look! There's a complimentary fruit bowl as well!"

I jumped down and sat by the low glass-topped table while Vino sighed theatrically and shook her head. The bowl was an eye-catching mix of colours and included both local and imported fruits.

"Oranges, guava, bananas, grapes, dragon fruit... I know we had a good lunch, but this is making my stomach growl again."

I tucked in while Vino also left the bed (more gracefully than I had, I admit) and hung her clothes in one side of the closet. As soon as she finished, I arranged mine into the space leftover and shut the double doors.

Vino gestured to the now almost empty fruit bowl. "You won't be able to swim with a full stomach."

"Nonsense! It's not that full!" I tucked in my stomach muscles to prove the point. "Anyway, I don't plan on training for the Olympics. I want to relax and let the water wash my stress away."

Not waiting for her answer, I grabbed my swimsuit and headed for the bathroom. A gentle scent of cinnamon greeted me when I opened the door. There was no tub (which was a pity since I love a good soak whenever possible) but it was spacious. I inspected the soaps and other free toiletries in glee. No mass-produced shampoos and lotions here. Everything was handmade locally using herbal products found in the area. The soap itself was a treat. It was cut off a larger bar and smelt good enough to eat!

"Yes!" I whispered to myself as I changed clothes. "I am definitely going to enjoy my stay here!"

The swimming pool was almost empty with only three other guests relaxing in the far corner when Vino and I entered. A couple were using the deck chairs under a large umbrella, and I could see some waiters moving around serving drinks from the bar. I gingerly stuck a toe into the water. It was lukewarm, just the way I liked it. I carefully descended the stairs, but Vino, showing off her athletic prowess, sat on the edge and took a shallow dive into the water. I had to admit she looked like a professional swimmer with her slim figure, long limbs, and no-nonsense swim wear. A couple of strokes later she was at the other end of the pool. I shook my head as I smiled at her. When you are five feet eight inches in height, and the pool is a mere fifty feet long, it doesn't take much to get to the other end.

Taking a deep breath, I swam leisurely to join my friend. Although I had swum regularly as my choice of exercise back in Colombo, it had been months since my last visit to this pool. And that was before the hotel changed owners. *'Don't dwell on it, Kiyama,'* I chided myself as I clung to the wall of the deep end.

A few laps up and down helped me to relax. The evening sun travelled towards the horizon and a slight breeze picked up. The shallow end had a corner set up like a jacuzzi and we sipped our cocktails as we enjoyed the moment.

I was at the deep end when the back of my neck prickled. I am not one to feel premonitions of any sort, but I could feel someone watching me. I glanced around and noticed two young men who had just stepped out of the main building. One was thin, dark, and had the physique of someone who spent hours at the gym while the other was heavier, fair, and bespectacled. They were both watching us.

I nudged Vino with my foot, leaned over and whispered, "We have an audience."

Vino hooked an arm around the metal steps on the side of the pool and swivelled gracefully so that she could observe the two men. "I think we have found Chris David and the other guy. What was his name?"

'Chamil something-or-other."

"Well neither of them catches my fancy," she said. "But you may find a new friend," she added before ducking underwater and swimming to the other end.

I grinned. Of course, neither of them caught her eye. She was not interested in men.

The fairer guy walked up to the edge of the pool and waved at me. "Hey!" he said. "Are you also here for the Mystery Event?"

"Yes, we are."

He checked his wristwatch. "Damn, there's not enough time for us to go back upstairs and change into our trunks." He extended a hand. "I'm Chris David, by the way."

I looked at his hand blankly. *Did he expect me to shake with my wet hands?* I waved a palm and said, "Sorry, don't want to splash you." Then, I kicked the wall behind me and swam to join Vino at the other end.

"He's a Forward Peter," I informed her once I surfaced. "Oh no, he's coming round to this side!"

"Let me see if I can guess your names," he said chirpily, as he made himself comfortable in a nearby deck chair. He looked off into the distance as if trying to recall the names in the list. "Is it… Monisha, Serena, Kay… there were two names starting with K… I'm bad with names. My parents did me a great favour when they named me Chris. Such an easy one to remember, don't you think?" He looked at his friend who was standing nearby. "Oh, and this is Chamil."

I gritted my teeth and pasted a fake smile on my face. *So much for a nice, relaxing dip in the pool! Why do I attract the weirdos?*

"Actually, it's time we went up to our room and got dressed. We need to prepare for a wedding!"

I could see Vino grinning like the Cheshire cat, out of the corner of my eye. I narrowed my eyes at her and gave her a warning look. Which she ignored.

"It's a pity you guys can't join us. Maybe tomorrow?" she said, fluttering her eyelashes.

I rolled my eyes. She was not even interested in guys and here she was putting on a show just to egg them on. And *I* would have to endure their advances. I kicked her under the water.

She grimaced for a moment and went on. "As Kiyama here just said, we do need to go up and get dressed, though." She climbed gracefully up the metal stairs like a fashion model exiting the water. I could see the guys eyeing her figure. I gritted my teeth. No way would I be able to make an exit like that. I clambered out as fast as I could, banging my knee on the metal in the process. I turned and grabbed a towel without looking at them.

"See you in a few hours," I muttered as I made my way towards the hotel.

"I remember that name. Kiyama. And your friend is…?" Chris called after us.

Vino turned and answered, "You'll find out at the wedding!" His laughter brayed after us as we made our way indoors.

CHAPTER THREE

BY **6:30 PM** we were primped, spruced, and ready to take on a murderer. Or a loud, offensive, and overbearing man who sounded like a donkey when he laughed. Vino, as usual, had apologized profusely with a twinkle in her eye for encouraging Chris David at the swimming pool. I just shrugged it off and decided to enjoy the night as much as I could.

My choice of wedding attire was a floor length dress in peacock blue, with a silver design on the border and bodice. Vino and I made a day trip to Colombo last week to pick out my outfit. I stored an entire wardrobe of evening wear (and other clothes I would not need in a small town) at my mother's house after I walked out after ten years of marriage. My mother was of the old school and believed that a cheating husband was something to be endured; especially when one is almost forty years of age and beyond the first flush of youth. She did not approve of my 'hasty' decision. Therefore, a flying visit was essential to keep the peace and I made doubly sure she was not at home to badger me when we arrived. After picking up a few items, we left as soon as we could so as not to tempt a chance encounter.

Although Vino had discarded all the unnecessary trappings of city life when she moved to Parkaduwa, she had retained one or two formal-wear outfits that she loved. She now looked resplendent in a burgundy and gold two-piece accompanied by elegant gold jewellery. The slim trousers and tunic cut short in front accentuated her lean figure. I felt a quick stab of jealousy when she finished styling her hair. *Kiyama, she's your best friend. And this is not a competition!*

"You will outshine the bride!" I said as we exchanged glances in the mirror.

"You do know this is not a real wedding, right?" she said with a smile.

"Yes, but still, you will be the best dressed in the room."

When she stood up, I laughed. "And the tallest and tower over all the men making their egos wither!"

She reached out to pat my unruly hair into place. "You don't look too bad yourself. Let's go get them!"

Cocktails served on the rooftop was to be followed by the main event on the lawn downstairs. About ten people were mingling and chatting as Vino and I entered. Tall cocktail tables draped in black and gold dotted the hall and waiters glided through the crowd, platters held aloft. Soft music played in the background and the leaves on the potted plants fluttered in the gentle breeze.

"We're lucky it's a calm night," I whispered as we showed our lanyards to a staff member at the entrance. "The last thing I need is my hair all mussed up in the wind."

"Your real names, please?" he inquired with a smile.

"Oh, sorry! I completely forgot that we had filled in our character names for the event!" Vino apologized.

"Vinodhini Dias and Kiyama Fernando," I added, and he ticked off our names dutifully.

"Please help yourselves. You can place an order with one of the waiters, or order from the bar," he said, leading us in. "Mr. Peiris will be here in a few moments, and he invited all the guests to become acquainted with each other."

"I like your character name," Vino commented, as we approached a table. I selected some hors d'oeuvres from a passing platter. "Beatrice. It's much better than mine. For some reason I felt like an Aurora today."

"The northern lights; they're spectacular, so you needn't excuse your choice of name," I reminded her. "I was feeling like Beatrice from Much Ado About Nothing. So, you can outshine the bride and I can be a nagging shrew!"

Vino giggled as she nibbled her mini bites.

I was about to try one of the hors d'oeuvres myself, when a loud voice just behind me turned my stomach sour.

"Well! It's nice to see you both fully clothed!"

Vino's eyes widened and I flushed.

"My, and don't you clean up real good!"

I shut my eyes and breathed deeply while counting to five. When I opened them Chris and Chamil had joined us at our table. Chris was in a full suit while Chamil was wearing a brightly coloured handloom sarong and shirt. They both sported lanyards around their necks. I hoped fervently that someone would strangle Chris with his.

"Let's see what you call yourselves." He reached for my lanyard, even as I stepped back in a futile attempt to protect my personal space, and held it up as he read aloud, "Beatrice." He then peered at Vino's chest and said, "Aurora. Nice to meet you,

Beatrice, and Aurora! I see you are the Mother of the Groom and you're one of the Bridesmaids." He waved his placard at our faces and said, "I'm Jaime Lannister, the Wedding Photographer, and this is Neymar Ronaldo, the Best Man."

I could feel Vino looking at Chamil in interest and groaned inwardly. She played basketball in university and is into sports, exercise, and healthy living.

"Hey, you into football?" she asked, cheerfully.

"Yes. You look like an athlete yourself," Chamil replied, as he moved around the table towards her. That, unfortunately, left me to deal with Mr. Obnoxious-fan-of-GoT.

Refusing to be drawn into a conversation about the Lannister family and his similarities with the famous swordsman, I changed the subject. "Do you know anyone else here?"

Chris shrugged. "No. I've already met the most interesting pair."

I rolled my eyes and hoped I did not have to put up with this drivel for long. Salvation came in the form of an elegant elderly couple who made a beeline to our table.

"Vinodhini Dias? Is that you?"

Vino, who had been enjoying a sporty conversation with Chamil, looked up in surprise.

The gentleman held out his hand, "Harold Malwatte. I am, or rather was, your uncle's lawyer."

Comprehension dawned on Vino's face as she shook hands excitedly. "Of course! I knew I'd heard the name somewhere before! How are you doing?"

I took the opportunity to detach myself from Cumbersome-Chris and said, "Hi, I'm Kiyama Fernando, Vino's friend. This table is getting rather crowded. Shall we move over there?"

Thankfully, Vino caught on and agreed with, "Oh yes, let's leave these guys to enjoy their drinks."

As we left, I swear I saw Chamil wink at me. Despite his abysmally poor choice of companion, he may not be that bad, after all.

As I followed Vino and the Malwattes to an empty table, a waiter materialized like magic with some glasses of wine, and I listened as Vino chatted about her late uncle.

"Uncle Ranjith always spoke highly of you. I'm so glad to bump into you like this!"

"We knew you were in the area, of course, since you took over the rubber plantation. It is wonderful that you decided to participate in this event, too" replied Mr. Malwatte. "And how is the plantation doing?"

"Oh, it was tough having to learn everything from scratch. I was able to modernize the accounting department, though!" Vino remarked, referring to her former job as an accountant in a leading firm in Colombo. "But I had a lot of help. The General Manager is quite easy to work with and he was a Godsend. We're doing quite well now."

She paused to catch her breath, and asked, "Are you still practicing in Colombo?"

"Thank goodness, no." It was Mrs. Malwatte who replied, placing a well-manicured hand on her husband's arm. "He's officially retired now. Which means that we have the time to travel and try unusual events like this!"

Mr. Malwatte smiled and said, "Unofficially, I am always available to help my friends and colleagues. So, please do not hesitate to ring if you need any advice."

Watching Vino's excitement at meeting these friendly faces from the past, my eyes pricked with tears. I could still recall her words about the spite and jealousy she had had to deal with after her uncle's death. She deserved happiness and to know that not everyone was against her.

Mrs. Malwatte turned her gaze towards me. She seemed a formidable woman. Her elegant hair and clothes hinted at a good sense of style, and her bearing was confident.

"Do you work with Vinodhini?" she inquired politely.

I smiled. "No, we were in university together. I'm staying with her for a short time and helping with the administrative work, but it's not a permanent thing."

I gestured towards her lanyard. "You're the Maid of Honour, I see. And you're a Groomsman."

They both laughed. "This entire role-playing thing is unexpected. We thought there'd be a script of some kind. That would have been easier. But the instructions were quite clear and those tips on how to drop clues and what kind of personality we are supposed to have were useful. I find I'm looking forward to the main event," confided Mr. Malwatte.

"With your experience as a lawyer, I'm sure you will untangle the clues and discover the killer in no time!" said Vino, smiling.

We were interrupted by the sound of metal tapping on glass. Someone at the front was calling for our attention. We dutifully turned. A portly man of about sixty years of age stood in the centre of the room. It must be the hotelier, Mr. Peiris. The young lady by his side was dressed as a Kandyan bride in full regalia. Her saree was heavily worked in gold thread, and she was bedecked in the hair ornaments and multiple necklaces that are traditionally part of the costume. I felt sorry for her – imagine having to carry all that weight for the entire night, and this was not even a real wedding!

Vino leaned over and whispered, "I hope they forced the guy playing the Groom to also wear the traditional garb! That poor girl. She'll have a helluva crick in her neck tomorrow!"

"They're probably paying very well…" I whispered back, "to make it worth her while!"

"Ladies and gentlemen!" started Mr. Peiris. "I'm Januka Peiris. Welcome to our first event here at The Falcon's Rest as we celebrate the launch of our new luxury boutique hotel. Many of you have already complimented me on the effective organization of this Murder Mystery Event. So, I think it appropriate to introduce to you the brains behind the whole thing – Ms. Lavanya Cooray – who will also be playing the Bride today. I will leave the instructions of the evening in her capable hands."

Lavanya Cooray stepped forward to a smattering of applause. "Thank you, Mr. Peiris. And hello everyone. This getup is not very comfortable so let's get a move on."

Vino nudged me.

I giggled into my drink.

"I am playing the role of the Bride because it is my murder you must solve, in today's game. I hope all of you had the time to peruse the dockets that were supplied when you booked in and you are carrying the card with the conversation topics for your characters to share. But remember, this game is all about improvisation and making stuff up as we go along. During the game, play close attention to what everyone says and learn what you can about the other players.

"Now this is of paramount importance - you *must* reveal *all* of the facts about yourself from your character and personality cards. If you're unsure what questions to ask, take one of your personality traits and turn it into a question. Most of you at this party will have a motive for killing me, which you'll need to reveal when I'm not around you."

She stopped and winked. "This task should be easy since most of you here like talking about me behind my back!" Everyone laughed at that one.

"After a while, I will drop dead. Please read the note in my hand. It will keep the story moving and turn the game into a scavenger hunt. You'll have ten minutes to gather up as many clues as possible that I've hidden by the poolside and around the lawn downstairs. The wait staff will be at hand to ensure you stay within the designated area and to help you if you need assistance. I won't be able to help you at that point because I'll be dead!"

We all laughed again, but it sounded rather strained now. Obviously, I wasn't the only one who found this levity about death a tad disturbing.

"You must gather as many clues as possible and recall the conversations you have had with the other characters to solve the mystery. When time is up, my spirit will arise to ask all the guests to point to whom they believe is the murderer. Afterward, the murderer will confess."

More applause.

A few of the guests began to chatter excitedly.

Mr. Peiris clapped his hands for attention and added," If you need any clarifications about the rules of the game, please stay back and have a chat with us. Otherwise, please make your way downstairs. Everything has been prepared on the lawn."

I glanced at Vino and the Malwattes and raised an eyebrow. "Anyone need clarification?"

"No, I'm good," said Vino.

The Malwattes also nodded their agreement, so we made our way to the exit.

I tried to suppress the hint of unease growing within me. It was probably a personal reaction to our previous negative experience at the hotel. Lightning did not strike twice, did it?

CHAPTER FOUR

DARKNESS WAS FALLING when we made our way to the ground floor. The sky was painted in gorgeous shades of purple and orange above the paddy fields which stretched into the horizon. The poolside and garden were already illuminated with massive lights, and the furniture and décor were arranged to resemble an outdoor wedding. There was an actual poruwa near the farthest boundary overlooking the paddy fields below. Fairy lights decorated the trees and shrubs. A long table for sixteen extended the length of the garden. Intricate table centres and expensive cutlery were in place.

"It looks like a *real* wedding," Vino murmured, as we stepped onto the grass.

My high heels immediately sank into the soft earth. "Let's stick to the flagstones," I said, as I yanked my foot out, "or I'll break my sandals!"

We made our way around the table trying to locate our places. Unfortunately, Vino and I had been separated and were assigned seats at either end. I was horrified to notice the name CHRIS DAVID on my left. Glancing around surreptitiously to ensure no one was watching, I swiped his card and exchanged it with another about three seats down. Vino saw my actions and wagged a finger in mock admonishment.

All the participants soon gathered. Lavanya Cooray waved her hands and called out, "Mingle, and remember the rules!"

I pulled my card out of the small clutch bag I was carrying, and read:

In this game, you are the Mother of the Groom. You designed and selected all the outfits and the décor for the wedding. Your favourite part of the wedding was the preparation.

Motive:
You don't approve of the Bride. You seriously consider killing the Bride at the party, but you decide against it.

Personality Traits:
☐ Drive an Audi
☐ Clumsy
☐ Camera Shy

☐ **Have a pet bird**
☐ **Once a dress designer**
☐ **Optimistic**
☐ **Kind of believes in the supernatural**

While Playing, Do This:
☐ **Compliment people's outfits**
☐ **Insist the Bride eats more**
☐ **Ask people for a loan**

"I wonder who the Groom is," I mused as I headed towards the nearest group of people.

"Hello and thank you for joining us on this happy occasion!" I said, as I joined them. "I'm Beatrice and I'm the Mother of the Groom."

I looked closely at each lanyard, but it was difficult to decipher some of the handwriting. "And you are?" I pressed on, turning to the gentleman on my right.

"I'm Steve. I'm one of the Groomsmen" he promptly answered offering to shake my hand. Then, dropping his voice he said," The actual name is Riaz, by the way. This is so confusing since everyone has two names, it's twice the effort to remember!"

"And I'm Hamzah. I decided to make life easy for everyone by just keeping my name. I'm a Guest," the lady wearing a beaded shalwar kameez and hijab next to Riaz said briskly.

Uh-oh, she doesn't sound happy to be here.

I looked at the last member of this small group, a plump blonde in a smart pantsuit.

"My real name is Megan," she said in a faint American accent, "but for the wedding I'm Roxanne. And I'm also just one of the Guests." She smiled at Hamzah, and added, "Honestly, it takes some of the pressure off, being such an insignificant character!"

We were joined by a young man carrying two cocktail glasses, one of which he handed to Megan. "Have you guys started without me?" he asked, in a broad American accent.

"Just introductions," Megan answered, slipping her hand into his. "This is Rob, my partner in real life. He's keeping his name, too. And he's the lucky Groom today!"

We all laughed politely.

"I'm so pleased to meet you," I said chirpily. "Although, ideally, I should be able to recognise my own son!" I consulted my card and asked, "So, what was your favourite moment of the wedding?"

"Oh, I almost laughed out loud when the Best Man couldn't find the rings!" said Riaz/Steve, with a grin.

"We couldn't see that from where we were sitting," said Megan/Roxanne, who seemed to be enjoying the playacting. She looked at me and asked, "What was your favourite moment?"

I consulted my card again and said, "I loved getting everything ready for this event. I designed all the outfits and décor, you know."

"That's fantastic!" Riaz/Steve exclaimed, fiddling with his phone. "I think we should take some photos of your outfit!" And he positioned himself to take a group selfie.

I quickly sneaked a glance at my card. *Drat!* It said I was camera shy. I took that as my cue to leave and said, "So sorry dears, but I'm really not that photogenic. Anyway, I need to go and mingle with the others," as I walked off.

Looking around, I noticed that Vino was talking to the Bride. I made my way towards them, tottering unsteadily as my high heels sank once more into the treacherous grass. When I drew nearer, I called out, "Hi darling! How's your big day going?"

They both turned to me in confusion, but Lavanya quickly caught on and answered, "Oh, my new Mom-in-law! There you are! The outfits and décor are great. Only thing is… I can't locate my husband!"

I looked at the group I had just left and said, "Rob's over there. He's enjoying the party, while you two are gossiping over here."

Vino giggled. I waved my character card at her and wiggled my eyebrows.

"You're a Bridesmaid, aren't you?" I asked her, feigning ignorance.

"Yes, Mrs.… erm… Beatrice," she faltered.

I turned to Lavanya and said, "You really should eat more, dear. Otherwise, you won't last the night!"

The double entendre was out of my mouth before I could stop myself, and we all laughed into our drinks.

Lavanya recovered first and replied, "Oh, don't worry. My friend Aurora here has been feeding me." She looked around at the other guests. "Have you spoken to everyone yet?"

I made a face. "No. This is taking a lot longer than I thought. And there is so much left in my card to reveal! It's quite hard, you know, just dragging random things into the conversation!"

Lavanya nodded. "Hmm… We had originally allotted half an hour for the chit chat, but I'd better hold off collapsing for a while longer then." With that, she excused herself and moved on to another group.

Saluting Vino with my half-empty glass I headed towards a group of three young girls who were sipping cocktails while perched on some deckchairs.

"Hello, I'm Beatrice and I'm the Mother of the Groom," I said when I got their attention. "I hope you're enjoying yourselves?"

"Oh yes, thank you," said one with long black hair in a French plait, and a deep green cold-shoulder dress. "I'm Serena. And this is Minosha, and Kumudu."

"Serena! You are supposed to use our character names!" giggled Minosha who sported a short pixie haircut. She was dressed in a sequined peach and black saree.

"Serena is already tipsy," commented Kumudu dryly, shaking her head. She wore thick dark-rimmed spectacles, and her hair was pulled back in a bun. Her choice of wedding attire was a power suit. "We decided to go as Ariana, Camila, and Billie."

"Lady Gaga, Pink, and Cardi B would have been too way out, you know?" commented Serena. She had a rather glazed look to her eyes, and I wondered how many drinks she had already had. *I hope she doesn't collapse before the end of the event!*

I did not recognize all the names but gathered they must be famous singers. Deciding to move things along, I peered at my card and asked, "I used to be a dress designer, and I must say you three really carry those outfits off!"

Minosha played with the tassels of her saree, but Serena fluttered her eyelashes and giggled, "Thank you so much! I do love to shop for new clothes!"

Kumudu sighed and rolled her eyes. "Serena seems to have forgotten that we're role playing," she explained. She looked at her own card and asked abruptly, "I'm the Wedding Planner. I hope everything is to your satisfaction?"

I smiled and played along. "Oh yes, you've done a marvellous job. I hope you like the outfits and décor. I selected them."

She glanced around and said, "Yes, very nice."

Minosha, who was also checking her card, jumped in with, "Does anyone have a pet?"

Blinking at the sudden change of topic, I answered, "Yes, I have a pet lovebird."

We looked at the other two, waiting for their responses. After checking her card, Kumudu said, "Pet Cat. Actually, I have some cute photos on my phone if you like to see?"

We all turned to Serena. She was peering under her deck chair. "I know I had that card here just now…" she mumbled.

I rolled my eyes and sincerely hoped Serena was not the murderer. If she were, no one would guess since she was not imparting any of the necessary information!

Hiding my irritation at irresponsible twenty-year-olds I took their leave.

I was relieved when, about twenty minutes and numerous awkward conversations later, Lavanya finally collapsed elegantly into a chair. I too grasped the opportunity to take a seat – my feet were killing me.

Everyone else crowded around the Bride with exclamations of surprise. Robert opened her clenched fingers and extracted a note which he read out dramatically:

"I know many of you dismiss my claims of supernatural powers, but I knew that I would die tonight. However, I will not let the murderer go free. So earlier, I hid slips of paper noting my psychic impressions throughout the garden. These will give clues as to who killed me. I will give everyone ten minutes to find the clues, and after that, my spirit will return and demand that each guest point to whom they believe murdered me in hopes the real murderer will confess. Those that guess correctly will be greatly rewarded.

Good luck!"

The silence that had fallen during the reading was broken by Mr. Peiris' voice calling out, "You may move around and look for the clues now!"

I groaned. I was in no mood to get back up.

"The Mother of the Groom is overcome with grief and unable to participate," I muttered to Vino as she joined me. "Seriously though, should we check if she's alright, and that this is definitely part of the game?"

"Oh, come on," she urged dragging me to my feet. "It's part of the game. Robert and the others around her would have noticed if something were wrong. Okay, we can pool in our finds. I'll walk around the garden while you check the dining table."

With that she was off.

I kicked my sandals off and lifted the hem of my dress to avoid grass stains. Then I leaned over the elaborate table centres, checking for clues. Astoundingly, I found two rolled up pieces of paper almost immediately. They said:

- **The murderer enjoys singing**

- **The murderer knows how to use a real gun**

However, try as I might, I could not recall anyone mentioning either of those in conversation. I walked slowly around the table checking under the placemats and lifting cutlery but to no avail. As I straightened up, I noticed that the other guests had dispersed in all directions. Vino was checking behind some bushes near the far fence. Megan and Robert were looking at the folded umbrellas over some deckchairs. Kumudu and Minosha were inspecting the poruwa. Deciding that the poruwa was the most likely place for more clues, I made my way towards the girls.

Since both Andy and I were Christians, we had had a traditional church wedding. I have many Sinhala Buddhist friends, so although I had not officially stood in one, I was no stranger to the Sri Lankan poruwa wedding ceremony. A poruwa is a beautifully decorated wooden platform with stairs on three sides and a canopy on top. The Bride and Groom stand inside surrounded by the officiant and their relatives. This poruwa was draped in fine white cloth and adorned in beautiful pink, white, and purple flowers and green creepers. There were fairy lights weaving between the natural elements providing a magical finishing touch.

I crouched beside a punkalasa that was on the bottom most stair on the right. The prosperity pot was full of coconut flowers and sheafs of golden rice paddy. My fingers between the stems closed on another roll of paper. *Yes!*

"Did you find anything?" It was Kumudu. She was kneeling by the other pot on the left.

Not wanting to lie, I answered, "Yes. What about you?"

"Minosha found a piece of paper tucked into the canopy. We haven't read it yet."

I looked around. "Where's Serena?"

Kumudu shrugged. "She was drunk. I told her to rest."

I laughed and shook my head. *Oh, to be young and carefree again!*

Gathering up my dress, I said, "I'll leave you to it then," and turned. The figures moving around the garden were indistinct. I could only recognize those who stood in pools of light.

Suddenly, the happy chatter was broken by a piercing scream.

CHAPTER FIVE

IFROZE. Surely the scream was part of the game? But shouldn't someone have screamed earlier when Lavanya had pretended to die? Minosha descended the wooden stairs and Kumudu stood up. All three of us peered into the darkness.

"Did you notice which direction it came from?" I asked them.

They both shook their heads and murmured, "No."

Vino hurried over to join us.

"I was in that far corner," she said, pointing to the right. "I thought the scream came from beyond me, from amidst the trees. It's not too well lit so I figured they must have not hidden any clues in the dark…" Her voice trailed away as someone ran to the centre of the garden. She had her hair covered – it was Hamzah. She stumbled as she almost collided with a dining chair. She was holding her hands outstretched before her. Even from this distance I could see that she was trembling.

"Riaz! *Riaz!*"

We all ran towards her. Her husband reached her first and caught her quivering body in his arms. Then he looked down at his shirt.

"Is that blood?" he yelped.

By this time everyone out on the lawn and by the pool had reached the couple. A babble of voices shouted.

"What happened?"

"Is she hurt?"

"Is someone else injured?"

I nudged Vino who was much taller than me. "What can you see?"

"She doesn't seem to be injured in any way. But she has something on her hands…" We exchanged concerned glances.

"Quick, take a head count. Is anyone missing?" I hissed.

Vino leaned left and right, peering through the crowd. Her lips moved as she silently counted.

"It's no use," she said at last. "There are too many people. The wait staff and even some of the kitchen staff seem to be here, in addition to the guests."

Mr. Peiris waved his arms and shouted, "Quiet!"

The sudden silence was eerie.

The calm before the storm.

"Guests, please take your seats at the dining table. Let's see if anyone is missing. Wait staff, spread out in that direction and look for whatever disturbed Ms. Hamzah," he ordered, pointing towards the trees. "Mr. Riaz, please bring her with me. I will show you to the nearest washrooms."

Hamzah shook her head vehemently. "I want to go back to our room. I've had enough of this charade!" She pushed her way through the crowd and ran towards the main building.

"Please, excuse us," Riaz muttered before dashing after her.

The remaining guests moved silently towards the long table. The warm night air felt oppressive, and the glare of the lights too bright on the eyes. I felt a tug on my arm. It was Minosha.

"Beatrice, Serena isn't here!"

It took me a moment to realise she was using my character name.

"Actually, my name is Kiyama. Are you sure she isn't asleep on one of the deck chairs? Maybe passed out from the drink?"

Minosha bit her lip and shook her head. Her eyes shone with unshed tears.

"Vino!" I whispered, as loudly as I dared. "Over here!"

She paused in mid stride and changed direction towards us. A few people already at their seats watched us curiously.

"Serena isn't here. Help us check all the deck chairs and the surrounding area. It's quite dark. She may have passed out beyond the lighted area."

Kumudu too joined us and the four of us weaved our way back and forth around the pool. We met again by the changing rooms.

"Anything?" I asked, anxiously.

The others shook their heads.

I gripped Minosha's hands. "Don't worry. She may have gone back up to your room to lie down. Why don't you run up and check?"

"Is everything alright?" A voice called from the dining table. It was Lavanya, 'risen from the dead.'

"Nothing to worry about!" I called back. "Minosha is heading upstairs to see if Serena is okay."

A commotion at the other end of the lawn caught our eyes. A member of the wait staff had burst into the light.

"She's dead!"

All hell broke loose.

Minosha wailed and collapsed into my arms.

I couldn't take her weight. "Help! Vino!" I gasped as I staggered towards a deck chair.

Kumudu had her palms on her face, her eyes wide and staring. Vino escorted her too towards a nearby deck chair.

At the dining table those who were seated leapt to their feet. I could hear Chris shouting something about fate (he sounded more excited than concerned). I heard the drawling accents of the two Americans and the firm voice of Tracy Malwatte commanding someone to 'put that damn phone down!'.

Leaving Minosha and Kumudu to huddle together, I stood up and looked across at the crowd. Two dining chairs were overturned. Everyone was milling around. Chris and Chamil had run over to speak to the waiter whose pronouncement had caught us all unawares. I felt Vino's hand on my arm.

"Come on," she whispered in my ear. "Let's find out what's going on."

We made our way around the pool and towards the voices raised in excitement. Mr. Peiris had returned. His face was grave. He whispered urgently to a staff member who raced off into the main building.

Chris saw us approach. "The missing girl is dead!" he said, his eyes shining.

He looked at us expectantly.

If he wants histrionics, he'll have to wait until kingdom come!

I ignored him and continued towards Mr. Peiris. His face was white, and his shoulders stooped. Gone was the confident, affable manner. I felt a surge of sympathy. *This place must be cursed!*

"Mr. Peiris," I said gently. "Why don't you come and sit down?"

"No… no…" he muttered, looking around vaguely.

"Please," I said, steering him towards the dining table. "If what Chris said is true and Serena is dead, there's nothing we can do about it but wait for the police to arrive."

Vino poured a glass of water and passed it to me.

"Here," I said, "drink this. It will make you feel better."

"I think we could all do with something much stronger than water!" said Chris, almost jovially.

That was the last straw. I had had enough of the clown. Turning, I grabbed him by his shirt and spat out, "Shut your damn mouth if you have nothing worthwhile to say! There's nothing enjoyable about this situation! The last thing we need is a herd of drunken idiots here when the police arrive!"

I felt someone gently prising my fingers open. Blinking, I recognized Chamil. Vino was on my other side. She escorted me to a chair, while Chamil took Chris to the opposite end of the table.

"Okay, Kiy, calm down," she said. "We're all wound up and upset. I'm not agreeing with what he said," she went on as I opened my mouth to object, "you were right, but we all need to take a deep breath now."

Accepting the truth of her words, I nodded and sat down. I watched as the Americans escorted Kumudu and Minosha back to their seats as well. The entire party was in place.

"Mr. Peiris," Vino continued, "could you please fill us in on what has happened?"

His head was in his hands. He looked up and surveyed the crowd. "There has been a terrible accident. One of our guests, I believe her name is Serena, is lying among the trees over there. She seems to have collapsed..." His stopped, unable to continue.

There was a long pause as everyone digested this.

Then a thought struck me. "Collapsed? Did anyone check if she's actually dead? Maybe she's just injured! Wasn't Hamzah covered in blood?"

Mr. Peiris shook his head. "We checked... She's..."

A murmur travelled around the table. We exchanged glances. An uncomfortable silence enveloped us broken only by Minosha's sniffs and sobs.

A quiet voice interrupted our private musings with, "Sir, shall I serve something to the guests?"

We all looked at the speaker in surprise. The Head Chef himself stood next to Mr. Peiris, his hands folded before him as if in supplication.

"Rohan!" said Mr. Peiris in obvious surprise. "You needn't have come out."

"That's alright, Sir. It's my pleasure. We have been preparing for this event for days. And it's getting late. I was wondering if we could start serving some of the food. I'm sure the guests must be hungry. It's almost 9 p.m. now."

Mr. Peiris looked at us, unsure.

Mrs. Malwatte must have picked up on his hesitancy because she immediately took command of the situation.

"Rohan, is it? Thank you so much for thinking of us. Yes, I think we would all like to eat something. We may be here for a while until the police give us permission to return to our respective rooms. Please, go ahead with the dinner as planned." She looked at us questioningly, "If that's acceptable to everyone?"

I could see relief on the faces of many as we all nodded. The nagging throb in my temples was a sign that I was famished, and I was looking forward to some food, despite the sombre circumstances.

"Yes, I will see to it immediately." With that, Rohan turned and walked briskly towards a side entrance of the building.

Within minutes the wait staff streamed out bearing dishes for our sit-down-dinner. The chef was obviously talented. The food was professionally plated and a feast for the eyes. It was also delicious. Although our mood was dampened by the tragedy, I noted how nobody declined to eat. The soup was creamy and lightly seasoned. The starter was an unusual combination of western and eastern flavours. The mains catered to both vegetarians and non-vegetarians in the group. The dessert was mouth-wateringly good. By the end of the meal, we were much more relaxed.

The wonders of good food!

It was only during the last course that it slowly dawned on me that there was a lot of activity at the far end of the garden. The police had arrived and started their investigation.

A familiar rotund figure in uniform made his way towards us. I hid my face in my hands and groaned. It was Inspector de Silva!

Vino noticed my reaction and patted my hand. "Don't worry, Kiy. He's not so bad, remember? And we're not to blame in any way, this time."

Megan, who was seated opposite us, leaned forward, interested. "This time? Have you had a run in with the cops before?"

I sighed. "It's a long story."

I kept my head down and urged Vino to do the same when Inspector de Silva approached the table. He cleared his throat. "Good evening, ladies and gentlemen. I regret having to impose on your dinner party, but murder is serious business."

"Murder!" Minosha broke in, her voice strained. "Are you sure? How can that be?"

"We are as sure as we can be right now. At first glance, the victim seems to have been strangled. We will know more once the forensic test results come in, Miss..." he looked at her questioningly.

"Minosha. Minosha Wijewardene."

"We would have started taking initial statements earlier, but your Head Chef insisted that we not spoil the meal," he went on, dryly. "He even went so far as to promise to feed me and my men. I gave some leeway, but now, we have a job to do."

"Inspector can't this wait until morning?" asked Mr. Peiris.

"Unfortunately, no, sir," came the answer. "We need to take down every detail while the memory is fresh. We will be back in the morning as well, so I urge you all to please speak to us if you remember anything new. But for now, I have some officers ready to take down whatever you have to say. Please cooperate with them and the sooner we finish the sooner you can all go to your rooms."

He gave a curt nod and strode off.

We looked at each other, waiting for someone to make the first move.

"Oh, what the hell," I said as I stood up. "Come on, Vino, let's go and say 'Hi' to the nice Inspector!"

The police had set up in the library on the ground floor. Four officers sat waiting for us at the four corners of the room. I glanced around as I entered. Inspector de Silva rose from his seat on my right.

"Miss Vinodhini and Miss Kiyama!" he exclaimed. "I didn't realise you were among the guests outside!"

"Yes," I said as I marched towards him and plonked myself down into the nearest armchair. "It's nice to keep bumping into you too!"

He grinned. "I should have known you two would be involved in some way."

"Involved?" I spluttered. "We bought tickets to participate in an event! Since when is that being 'involved'?"

"Calm down, Miss Kiyama," he offered, raising a placatory hand. "I meant no harm by the comment. But you two do have a knack for being in the wrong place at the wrong time. Or is it the right place at the right time, ah? Truth be told, your insights may be helpful. Plotting the movements of fifteen guests and God-only-knows how many staff is not going to be easy. But you two are observant. I know from our previous encounter that you have a nose for these things."

I sniffed, mollified. "How can we help?"

He gestured for Vino too to take a seat. Then he turned to the other three officers. "Can you find another empty space to conduct your interviews, please? This may take a while. And I don't want the other guests to notice that these ladies are getting special treatment."

Turning back to us, he asked, "So, from the beginning please. Take me through the day."

I sighed. Yes, this was definitely going to take a while.

It was close to midnight when Vino and I finally reached our hotel room. Everyone else seemed to already be in bed: we could see no lights shining through the doors of our neighbours' rooms. We were knackered. Inspector de Silva had taken us over our story what felt like a million times. Every little detail, smell, and sound had been noted and discussed. It is surprising what the human brain retains in its subconscious.

"You know," I said, my mouth widening in a jaw breaking yawn, "I didn't realise that I hadn't spoken to some of the guests during the game. It's not like I was avoiding anyone…"

She gave me a look.

"Okay, okay. So, I was actively avoiding the donkey, but I was trying to follow the rules of the game and impart all my information. Did you speak to him?"

She grinned. "I spoke to Chamil…"

I snorted. "Of course you did! If you were not a confirmed lesbian, I would have assumed there was a spark there!" I paused as a new thought struck me. "Does he know? About your preferences, I mean?"

Vino nodded as she grabbed a towel and headed for the bathroom. "I told him. I didn't want to lead him on. He's okay with it."

I fell into the closest armchair. "Hey, maybe I should tell Chris that I'm les too. He might leave me alone then."

She gave me a sceptical look. "I trust Chamil to keep his mouth shut. He doesn't seem the type to natter unnecessarily. Chris, on the other hand, may start cracking inappropriate jokes and that could lead to unpleasant rumours. You know how it works. We do have to live in this small town after they leave…"

She locked the door and I leaned back into the soft cushions. My entire body ached, and I had blisters on my feet. I smiled to myself. I had realized I was barefoot halfway through the interview with the Inspector and had to run out and search for my discarded sandals before the garden lights were turned off for the night. Fortunately, Inspector de Silva was by now accustomed to my little idiosyncrasies and had not read anything ominous into the sudden departure.

He should thank his lucky stars that we were reliable witnesses to the evening's happenings. It also meant that he had two people less to suspect – thirteen possible killers was quite enough to get on with, and that was discounting the hotel staff who had also been present throughout the evening.

It was quite an intriguing puzzle. Other than Vino and the Malwattes, no one else had mentioned any previous connection to each other. I did not know everyone's backgrounds, yet. We would have to start with Serena and her friends. The first thing to do tomorrow was to speak to the two girls. They had turned to us tonight in their time of need and we could capitalize on that.

My eyes felt heavy, and I yawned once more. The Inspector had left us with a firm warning not to interfere, but my nose was twitching. We were slap bang in the middle of another murder inquiry. And I could not just let go.

CHAPTER SIX

I AWOKE THE next morning with a massive crick in my neck. I could barely remember changing out of my evening wear and getting into bed. Vino, who was always up at dawn, was bright eyed and bushy tailed. As for myself, sluggish was the politest term my befuddled brain could conjure.

I was rudely thrown about when Vino climbed onto the bed with two steaming mugs of Nescafe in hand. She waved one under my nose and sang, "Sha-la-la-la-la-la Live For Today…"

I groaned and muttered, "It is *not* a Good Morning world…" as I pulled the covers over my head. The chirpy advertisement was the last thing I needed.

"Besides," I continued, trying to ignore the tantalizing fumes, "I prefer real coffee… ground coffee. And, considering the events of last night, 'Live for Today' is just about all we can do…"

"I know, but this is what we have in the room. I'm sure they have a better blend downstairs. Don't be so grumpy! Just drink this. It'll wake you up."

She extended one cup towards me again and I surrendered. Rubbing my gritty eyes, I sat up and took a sip. It wasn't that bad.

"So, what's the plan?" Vino demanded, while I struggled to defog my mind.

"Plan?"

"Yes! Last night you muttered something about Minosha and Kumudu when I woke you up. You were snoring in the armchair, by the way."

"I do not snore!"

"Grunting, then. Anyway, you washed and changed in a daze, I think. Are you thinking of investigating this?"

"It makes sense, doesn't it?" I said, my mind finally kicking into gear. "We already know the guests. And they're more likely to share with us than with the police. We'd be helping the cops! We can pass on anything significant we find."

As if on cue, the phone rang.

I answered it. "Hello?"

"Good morning. Is that Miss Kiyama or Miss Vinodhini?" said a voice. I recognized the receptionist who had served us yesterday.

"This is Kiyama," I replied.

"I hope I did not disturb you, but Mr. Peiris would like to meet you both privately either during or after breakfast."

I covered the mouthpiece and passed on the message to my friend.

"During," she whispered back.

"Sure," I spoke into the phone. "We'll speak to him during breakfast. We can be down in about half an hour."

I replaced the receiver thoughtfully. "I wonder what he wants."

Vino bounced off the bed. "Well, you have half an hour to get dressed! And then we'll find out!"

Breakfast was served buffet style in the Breakfast Room on the ground floor. I glanced around as soon as we walked in. Most of the other guests were already seated. The Malwattes and the Americans were serving themselves. Chamil and Chris were eating at one table and Hamzah and Riaz were at another. Mr. Peiris and Lavanya were at a table set for four in the far corner.

Mr. Peiris rose as we approached. "Good morning, ladies. Please join us."

He gestured for a waiter. "Tea or coffee?"

"Coffee, please," we chorused.

He and Lavanya were in the middle of their meal. He gestured towards the buffet and said, "Please, serve yourselves. And then we'll have a chat."

I selected kola kanda, muesli and some fruit while Vino opted for the Full English Breakfast.

"Sha-la-la-la-la-la Live For Today..." she sang when I raised an eyebrow.

We settled down and looked inquiringly at the owner of the hotel. He looked more like his usual self this morning. A good night's sleep had obviously been beneficial.

"Forgive me if I am curious," he started, "but, is it true that you solved a murder a few months ago?"

I froze with the spoon halfway to my mouth. *Who had told him that?*

"Yes," I said, cautiously.

"That's fantastic!"

Vino and I exchanged a startled glance.

"Of course, no murder at all is better but, what I meant was… would you be willing to take on this case as well?"

"Take on this case?" I echoed. "We're not private investigators. We got involved last time against our wills, really. And I don't know how the police would feel…"

I knew jolly well how the police would feel!

"Why do you want us to investigate, Mr. Peiris?" Vino asked.

He squirmed a little in his seat, and his face turned a darker shade of brown. "Well, I don't want to speak ill of the police, but this is a small town, not Colombo. We don't know how competent they are. I would feel better if a second set of eyes and minds were working in the background. Also, we just opened the hotel. Bad publicity is the last thing we need! We're moving into the end-of-year holiday season, and we need people to feel safe and comfortable here. We can't afford to lose customers!"

I felt obliged to point out that the Eheliya police were not that bad. "Actually, Inspector de Silva is very competent. We were impressed with his work ethic last time, weren't we, Vino?"

"Definitely," she agreed. "We had our doubts, but he proved us wrong."

"That may be, but I'd feel better if you could do this for me," insisted Mr. Peiris.

"Can we discuss this, please?" I requested, rising. I tilted my head towards the buffet table. We picked up a plate each and moved towards the deserted salad bar.

"What do you think?" I muttered.

"Isn't this what you want?" she countered.

"Yes…" I said hesitantly. "To quietly speak to everyone to satisfy my own private curiosity is one thing, to be officially hired by the hotel management is quite another!"

"Oh, come on," disagreed Vino. "The guests will be wanting to leave. Although this is a long weekend and tomorrow is Poya, the police can't make people stay. And I doubt the hotel would offer free accommodation to the guests indefinitely until the murder is solved. So, we're on the clock, in a manner of speaking. Two heads will definitely be better than one! Also," she continued. "You're not one to refuse a challenge. And, think of this, we can get paid for snooping!"

"Getting paid! How much should we quote if he asks us to name our price?"

"I don't know… maybe free use of the pool and spa for life?"

I laughed. "That's a brilliant idea!"

By the time we served our salad and moved back to our table, Lavanya and Mr. Peiris had finished their meal and were awaiting our decision. He looked at us hopefully.

"Yes," I smiled. "We'll help. But there's no guarantee of success."

Waving the last comment away he said, "Fabulous!" and rubbed his hands together. "About payment…"

"Oh, we don't need cash. But we do have an alternative proposal. Would you be willing to allow us unlimited use of your pool and spa?" I crossed my fingers under the table.

"Unlimited use of the pool and spa?" Mr. Peiris looked shocked. This was obviously unexpected. Then he nodded, thoughtfully. "Alright. The pool I can allow. But shall we say access to the spa if and when in-house guests are not using it?"

"It's a deal!"

We shook on it.

"So, tell me what you need from me," he said, as a waiter cleared away their plates.

"Don't tell the other guests we've been hired to investigate this," I instructed him promptly. "We can just chat with them and steer the conversation as the need arises. Some may be open to sharing and others not so much. Don't tell the staff either. We may be able to find out details they don't wish the authorities to know in casual conversation. People tend to clam up when the police come calling."

"Also, you will have to allow the guests to stay on tomorrow as well if they haven't booked the extra day," added Vino. "Maybe give a discount or something."

He nodded. "The police have already requested that."

A thought occurred to me. "What do we tell the police?"

"I think we should tell them the truth," suggested Vino. "After all, we don't want to get in trouble with Inspector de Silva." She turned to Mr. Peiris. "Last night, he warned us not to get involved. Perhaps you could tell him you've hired us to work independently on this? And please request that he share anything significant they discover through their forensic tests."

"Yes. I will ring him up from my office. Anything else?"

"Mr. Peiris, as a matter of form, could you tell us what you saw and heard last night?" I inquired.

"Me? Why? Am I a suspect? I wouldn't kill a guest and sabotage my own event!"

"You aren't a suspect, Mr. Peiris, you're a witness," I said, soothingly. "We'll be asking this from everyone. We need to make a note of everyone's movements throughout the event."

Vino nodded encouragingly.

"I'll go first," Lavanya offered. "Once we were all in the garden, I mingled playing my role as the Bride. I spoke to both of you, remember? And I made sure to interact with all the others as well."

"What were your impressions of Serena?" I asked.

"She seemed to be enjoying herself!" Lavanya laughed. "And you can't fault that. You are young only once!"

"What about you, Mr Peiris, did you mingle as well?"

"No. I didn't take a character card since I wanted to be free to ensure everything ran smoothly," he said. "I watched the waiters, checked how things were going at the bar, and so on. Then I took a break at the dining table."

"After Lavanya's 'death' did you both stay put at the table?" Vino asked.

"Yes. We hid the clues, so it was entertaining to see how everyone was faring with the scavenger hunt," said Mr. Peiris.

"Do you remember seeing anyone walk towards the side garden where Serena was found?"

"No…" he admitted.

Lavanya too shook her head. "I was playing dead!"

I sighed. "It's okay. There were so many people wandering around, and it was dark. I just hope we find someone who saw something."

"What's your official post here, if you don't mind me asking?" Vino turned to Lavanya.

"I was hired to organize this event."

Mr. Peiris stood up. Lavanya joined him.

"We'll leave you to enjoy the rest of your meal," he said. "Keep me informed about any developments."

Waiting until they had left, I turned to Vino. Her eyes were glowing. She looked as excited as I was.

"Kiyama and Vino, Private Investigators!" I said.

"No. V & K Associates!"

"You lose it: We find it!"

"You kill it: We catch you!"

I pulled a face. "Er… definitely not!"

Vino shrugged. "You kill: We fulfil?"

I shook my head. "Let's just focus on the case."

"Hide your face: We're on the case!"

"Vino!"

After the hearty breakfast we decided to check in on Minosha and Kumudu who had not been down all morning.

"Hi," I greeted the receptionist as we entered the lobby. "We want to see how Minosha and Kumudu are doing. Can you please tell us their room number?"

She hesitated. "Actually, Miss, with all that's happening, I don't know if I should…"

I looked at her blankly for a moment before it dawned on me. "Of course. Better be safe than sorry with a killer on the loose. But don't worry. We mentioned it to Mr. Peiris during breakfast just now. It was the other receptionist who called our room, but you know he wanted to meet us, right?"

She smiled and nodded. "Yes. I'll check with Mr. Peiris but you can go up. They are sharing Room 201. They booked the suite."

"That's on our own floor. Thank you. Oh, and Lihini" I added, reading her name off the tag on her blouse, "You're doing an amazing job!"

"We should ask Mr. Peiris to give us a guest list with the room allocations," Vino commented as we disembarked from the lift, "in case the next receptionist on duty is as conscientious as this one. It'll save on time!"

An eerie silence enveloped us as we made our way down the carpeted corridor.

"Perhaps everyone else is downstairs?" I whispered.

We reached Room 201. I kept my ear to the door.

"There's no noise," I noted. "Perhaps they slept in?"

Vino consulted her watch. "It's past ten o'clock! Surely, they must be awake by now."

"They're twenty-something year old girls. On holiday. Or maybe they were awake through most of the night worrying about Serena and they're finally getting some sleep."

Vino knocked.

No response.

She knocked louder.

"Should we alert Mr. Peiris? Could something have happened to them too?" she asked.

We were turning away when the door opened a crack.

"Who's there?" came a tremulous voice.

"Minosha? Is that you? It's Kiyama and Vino," I said.

"Yes."

The door opened wider.

"Can we come in? We just want to check on how you two are doing. Have you ordered room service? They're clearing up the breakfast buffet downstairs."

She stepped back and let us through. "We just woke up. I haven't even thought of food. I don't think I can…"

The room was much larger than ours. There was a king size bed on the left and a smaller single bed on the right. The cupboard, desk and chair were similar to ours, as was the décor. The balcony was bigger with two large armchairs outside.

Kumudu was staring blankly ahead, seated in the larger bed, her knees drawn up to her chin. Minosha joined her and buried her head in her hands.

I squirmed inside. I was not particularly good at this kind of thing. I gave Vino a nudge and mouthed, "Say something!"

She perched on the edge of the bed and put an arm around Minosha, who was sobbing quietly. I walked around to the other side and laid a hand gingerly on Kumudu's shoulder.

The silence stretched for eons.

Vino and I locked eyes above the girls' heads. I widened my eyes and lifted my eyebrows. Vino shook her head in response. I could feel Kumudu's shoulder trembling under my palm.

Finally, she burst out, "I can't believe this is happening! We were supposed to be enjoying a girls' weekend out!"

"How long have you known Serena?" I asked, quietly.

"We were in school together and kept in touch afterwards. It's not as easy to meet up now with work commitments and all that."

I pulled up a chair and sat next to her. "Are either of you married?"

Kumudu snorted. "No! We're only twenty-three!"

"Okay. Do you all work?"

"What's with all the questions?" she snapped. "We went through that with the police last night!"

Why was she so defensive? Was it merely grief… or something else?

I lifted my hand and backed down. "Nothing. We're simply curious about what happened. And why someone would want to do something like that. We'd like to help you in any way possible." I paused. "Don't you want to know?"

"Isn't it the job of the police to find out?" she countered.

"Yes," I acknowledged. "But we'll all be here for only one more day. Do you seriously think the cops can solve this in one day?"

She shrugged. "Maybe not. But what can we do?"

"Vino and I thought we'd speak to everyone privately. See if anyone saw anything. You sometimes remember little things hours later."

"How do you know that? Are you a cop too?"

I laughed. "No, of course not! I just love reading murder mysteries! So, what do you say – are you willing to talk to us and help us sort this out?"

Kumudu looked across at Minosha who had remained silent during this exchange. "Mino? What do you say?"

She shrugged noncommittally. "Whatever."

Vino rose and reached for the phone. "I think we need to order some food and drink before we get down to anything serious. These two need to keep their strength up."

While she ordered a full breakfast, I asked, "So, who do you think killed the Bride?"

Both girls looked at me in surprise.

"You know, the event. We were collecting clues, remember? Who do you think was the murderer of the Bride?"

Minosha giggled. "This is surreal. A murder within a murder!"

"I have to admit, I was expecting something to happen to Lavanya. I mean she kept talking about dying and that's what usually happens in books and movies, right?" I said.

"I'm glad that I wasn't the only one uncomfortable with the whole thing," Kumudu admitted.

"So," I said, returning to the original questions, "who do you think did it?"

"We're still talking about the event, right?" Kumudu asked.

"Of course."

"I talked to as many people as I could in the allotted time, and I think it was the Groom. The slips of paper we found said the killer drives an expensive car, but doesn't have a pet, and that fit what Robert said."

"What did our slips of paper say, Vino?" I asked.

"I can barely remember! Let's see… there was something about singing… yes! It said the killer liked to sing and also knew how to use a gun!"

We all frowned in thought.

After a moment I sighed. "Honestly, I can't recall all the conversations now. That's why you're supposed to complete the event in one go. It was an innovative idea though. Pity someone took advantage of the game and committed a real murder."

Another long and uncomfortable silence followed. I mentally kicked myself for leading us back to that. Fortunately, there was a knock at the door.

"Oh wonderful! The food is here!" I said chirpily and ran to accept the trays and then helped the girls settle down at the desk.

"I'm famished!" Kumudu exclaimed as she tucked in.

Minosha nodded. "I didn't realise how hungry I was until I saw this."

Vino and I maintained a low profile until they had finished. Once the last crumb had disappeared, I asked, "Do you feel better now?"

"Definitely!" they both chorused.

"Shall we go downstairs to the library? Or out onto the lawn? Get some fresh air?"

Kumudu smiled. "Alright. But I haven't even brushed my teeth for the day! And I'm sure we both look frightful. Give us some time to freshen up and we'll meet you on the rooftop. Is that okay? I don't want to face the crowd downstairs yet."

I nodded. "I totally understand. We'll be in our room. It's number 204. Give us a ring when you're ready and we'll meet you there."

"Minosha seems really distraught," I commented as we made our way back to our room. "But Kumudu is either a really cool character, or she was not as close to Serena as she claims."

"I think she's one of those highly intelligent, logical people. She was quick to question our motives, while Minosha just accepted what we said," Vino pointed out.

"So, partner," I quipped. "How do you want to go about this?"

Vino raised an eyebrow.

"Do we make a list of questions, or wing it?"

"I think we need to find out as much as we can about Serena. These two are the only ones who knew her well."

"Other than the murderer," I said.

"Other than the murderer," she conceded. "I highly doubt this was a random killing. You know what they say about looking at the near and dear ones first in situations like this. We need to figure out why she was killed. Whether she knew anyone else here. Everything Serena talked about this weekend, even in passing."

"Right."

I crossed to the desk and pulled out the complementary notepad and pencil and quickly jotted down everything Kumudu and Minosha had said during our conversation. Then, I tucked the stationery away in my bag.

"I doubt if Inspector de Silva is going to share all his information with us," I said, "so we need to find out where everyone was during the event. Between our own recollections and those of the others I'm sure we can draw up a timeline."

Vino shook her head. "How are we going to talk to twelve or thirteen people in one day? Keeping track of everything is going to be a nightmare!" She gestured towards my bag. "Surreptitiously keeping notes is not going to be easy. I think we should have asked for more than pool and spa privileges. This is going to be like digging an elephant's grave with a teaspoon!"

CHAPTER SEVEN

WE MET KUMUDU and Minosha at the lifts, and unanimously decided to take the stairs instead. The third floor housed the gym, spa, and rooftop lounge. We waved at Chamil who was using one of the machines in the gym and made our way out.

The view was breath-taking. I had not noticed it last evening, preoccupied as I was by the event. Being over thirty feet above ground level in a landscape devoid of any other buildings made for a fantastic panorama. All four of us walked out into the open area, concerns of murder forgotten amidst the beauty of our surroundings. A lone tree stood tall in the centre of the paddy fields while scarecrows grinned at each other, flapping black rags. The hills in the distance were hazy with far-off rain. The Parkaduwa Central college stared back at us, austere and white, from across the fields. I spotted the mud huts of the farmers nestled in one corner, and the garish billboard which stood out like a bruise on the otherwise serene countryside.

"I think I see our house," Vino whispered at my elbow. "Over there."

The wind tugged at our clothes as we eventually settled down beneath a wide canvas canopy. A small bar counter was set up in a sheltered corner and manned by one waiter who walked over, menu in hand, when we were ready to order.

"Tea and coffee can be served immediately, but other food and drink needs to be brought up from the main restaurant downstairs," he informed us.

Vino and I decided on coffee while the girls ordered smoothies.

"Would you like something to eat as well?" he inquired.

"No, thanks," I declined.

We got down to business once the waiter left.

"I know this must be hard on you, but can you please tell us something about Serena?" I started. "She was already quite tipsy by the time I spoke to you last night, so I was unable to get to know her at all."

Minosha fiddled with the hem of her blouse. She was dressed in a kurta top and pants. "She was so vibrant and full of life. She was always game for anything. She didn't care what anyone thought of her and lived life the way she saw fit."

"She sounds like a very confident young lady," I said.

"Hmph," said Kumudu, cutting in. "She had no idea of how to adjust to a situation, how to play her cards carefully. She expected everyone to accept her as she was, and that's fine, but…"

She stopped as Minosha cut in. "How can you say that? She was a lovely person! A good friend!" And she burst into tears once more.

Kumudu sighed. "She was my friend too. But you need to have some tact if you're going to get along with others. Serena wanted others to always bow to her will… She was headstrong in school, but it got worse after she started working at her father's company. I'm sure you've heard of it – Kumana Holdings?"

Vino's eyes widened, and I nodded as I recognised the successful business in Colombo. So, Serena came from a wealthy family.

Minosha shook her head, refusing to accept what was being said.

"What did she do in the company?" Vino asked, gently, trying to diffuse the situation.

"She was head of marketing." Kumudu's voice was tight.

I wondered whether she did not believe Serena deserved the position. I tried my luck. "At only twenty-three?"

"She did a diploma in marketing. And she was reading for a BA too..." Kumudu broke off, but I picked up on the subtext, which confirmed my suspicions.

"That's quite a responsibility to bear at a young age," I prompted.

"Oh, she had experienced staff under her," Kumudu said, offhandedly.

Kumudu's reaction was interesting. *Could there be bad blood between the two girls?*

"And what do you do?" I asked her.

"I'm reading for a degree in bioscience. Minosha is working as an accountant while completing her studies."

"Wow!" I exclaimed, genuinely impressed.

"Erm, did she like to drink a lot?" asked Vino. "It's just that, like Kiyama mentioned, she was too tipsy to hold a proper conversation last night."

"She liked to have a few cocktails, but she rarely got sloshed," said Minosha. "But then, we haven't been out of Colombo together in such a long time and she may have had more than usual..." Her voice trailed away, and I could see tears fill her eyes again. "Oh my God, who's going to tell Uncle and Aunty? I won't be able to look them in the face again after this!"

"Don't worry about that," Vino advised, taking her hand. "That's the job of the police. I guess it's good that neither of you called her parents last night. Breaking news like this is better left to the professionals...but..." She broke off and swallowed hard. "You'd better be ready to receive lots of calls from Serena's family and friends. Once they hear the news, they'll want to know what happened..."

I had not thought of that. These poor girls would have to field questions from all and sundry for the next few days.

Minosha looked horrified.

Kumudu just nodded grimly.

"When did you arrive for the Event? Did Serena speak to anyone other than you two? Did she know anyone else?" I asked.

"Well, we checked in on Friday just before lunch. We arrived a day early to enjoy the long weekend. I'd just finished some exams and I was keen to get out of Colombo. So were the others," Kumudu replied. "Anyway, on Friday we ate at the buffet and spent the afternoon in our room. Late evening, we drove to a gem museum nearby. We didn't buy anything, but Serena purchased a lovely pendant."

"And that night?"

"We had dinner here and watched a movie in the room. It's not as if there are any night clubs or anything out here!"

I let the sarcastic comment pass.

"Were any of the other guests here on Friday?"

Kumudu chewed on a nail as she thought. Then, she snapped her fingers and said, "Yes! The Americans were here!" She turned to Minosha. "That was the night of the argument, right?"

I sat up. "Argument?"

"Yes, Serena thought Robert was cute and flirted a little with him at the bar after dinner. His girlfriend didn't like it and made some snide remarks."

"Was that the first time you'd met them?"

Kumudu looked at me disdainfully. "They're here on a trip from the States. So, yeah, they were total strangers." She exchanged a smile with Minosha. "He *is* kind of cute. I remember Serena joking that she wouldn't mind meeting him again, alone."

She gasped and covered her mouth with her hand. "Is that what happened? She tried to seduce him, and his jealous girlfriend killed her?"

"Let's not get carried away here," I warned. "We don't even know how she died. Remember how we thought the red stuff on Riaz's clothes was blood? And then the cops said she was strangled? It's unlikely that a woman of Megan's size could strangle Serena, if that's what happened. Let's wait for the police to update us. We don't want to start idle speculation and rumours."

Minosha was hugging herself tight. I felt sorry for her.

"Did anything else happen on Friday night?"

They both shook their heads in denial.

"Okay. What happened on Saturday?"

"We woke up late. Had breakfast. Pottered around. Then we explored the hotel and the grounds in the evening. To be honest, it was dead boring waiting for the event to start."

"Didn't you want to use the pool?"

"No, Serena didn't want the chlorine in her hair before the event."

I laughed. "Why didn't I think of that? We would have not met Chamil and his donkey then!"

The girls looked puzzled.

Vino filled them in. "We went down to the pool at about four o'clock. Chamil and Chris turned up and, well, Kiyama found Chris rather annoying…"

They giggled. "His laugh does sound a bit like a donkey braying, doesn't it?" said Minosha shyly.

"Did you bump into any of the guests, you know, in the lifts or during your walk?"

Kumudu shrugged. "We passed a few people, but we didn't stop for a chat. We only met everyone officially at the rooftop later when the Mystery Event started."

It sounded like the three of them had kept mostly to themselves prior to the event.

"Okay, at what time did you get up here for the cocktails?"

"We came in last; I think. The owner of the hotel launched into his welcome speech a few minutes after we entered. We stood at an empty table and had a few snacks and some wine. Then, we followed the crowd back down."

"You didn't speak to anyone while the refreshments were being served?"

"No."

"So, what happened after you came to the lawn?" I asked.

"We spoke to the old couple first," started Kumudu.

"The Malwattes?" asked Vino.

"Actually, Serena was rather rude to them, which is quite unlike her. It may have been the drink. Then we spoke to the Muslim couple, Hamzah and what's-his-name."

"Riaz."

"Yeah. By then Serena couldn't walk so we took a break by the pool. Then you came along, and we had a chat."

"Then she must have had quite a few drinks on an empty stomach," I commented. "Did you go your separate ways at any point?"

They looked at each other.

"I went to the loo once. So did Kumudu," said Minosha. "But we made sure one of us was always with Serena given her condition."

"What happened after I left you?"

"Chamil and Chris sat down with us, and we played our parts for the game. Then the Bride collapsed. Everyone gathered around. Robert read out the death note. And we moved off to look for clues."

"Wait," I said. "Only both of you were at the poruwa. Why wasn't Serena with you?"

"She said her head was spinning and she wanted to lie down on a deck chair, so we left her there." Minosha's voice broke, and she curled in on herself even more. "We should not have left her there…"

I put an arm on her shoulder and said, "There's no way you could have known what was going to happen. You can't blame yourself. You're all grown-ups now. You didn't need to babysit her." I paused. "We need to find out why she left her place by the pool."

"Is there anything else you remember?" I pressed.

They shook their heads.

"Okay," said Vino. The waiter had arrived with our orders, finally. "Let's just relax now. But there is one thing you can do. Talk to everyone. Find out if they saw Serena after the death note was read. Someone must have seen something."

Having convinced Kumudu and Minosha to use the pool and relax, Vino and I strolled through the hallways hoping to bump into some of the other guests. We struck gold in the library. Hamzah, Riaz and the Malwattes were all taking a break among the books.

The library at the Falcon's Rest was quite impressive. Three sides were lined with colourful publications showcased in wooden bookcases built into the walls. There were bookish themed memorabilia everywhere. Scented candles bearing famous quotations were placed strategically on each desk and posters of book covers were mounted on the walls. There were even throw pillows with slogans such as 'Just One More Chapter' on the couches and armchairs that looked comfy and inviting. It was my kind of place. I longed to snuggle up with a bestseller and a cup of coffee. Instead, Vino and I prepared to interview more suspects. We decided to start with Hamzah and Riaz since we had barely spoken to them last night.

"Hi, Hamzah," I said as we approached. "How are you doing?"

She looked up from a magazine she was flipping through. "Fine."

"Listen," I continued as we dragged two seats up. "I'm dying to know… Was that blood, or something else like wine, on your hands last night?"

Riaz hiccoughed, and I saw he was struggling not to laugh out loud.

Hamzah gave him a cold look and said, "It was red wine. But I didn't notice that it was too wet to be blood at the time, okay, I was more preoccupied with the dead body!"

"I can imagine," commiserated Vino. "I don't know what I would have done if I had stumbled across her like that in the dark."

"Was it very dark in that part of the garden?" I asked. "You see, we didn't go that way."

"It was quite dark. The floodlights were in the main area by the pool." She shrugged. "Everyone was spreading out, so I just walked that way to escape the crowd."

Vino and I hung onto her every word, so she continued. "Actually, I wasn't interested in finding clues. Riaz is a great fan of mystery and suspense, and he was keen on the game, but I came on this holiday to relax, you know. We're newly married and I want to enjoy what free time I have before the kids arrive. I thought I'd wander around a bit and enjoy some quiet time. I barely saw her on the ground. She was wearing a green dress, right?"

We answered in the affirmative.

"She blended in with the grass and shrubs. I literally stumbled onto her. I tripped over her feet and threw out my hands to break the fall. That's when I got the wine stains on them. The grass was wet with it as if someone had spilt an entire glass. It was all over her body, too. Of course, at the time I thought it was blood. I shook her, but her eyes were open, and she wasn't breathing. I just panicked and ran back towards the lights."

"You were so brave," Vino said. "I would have fainted dead away on the spot." She stopped and giggled. "Oops, bad choice of words!"

I grimaced. And, Vino had the temerity to call *me* dramatic!

"When did you realise it was just wine?" I asked.

"When I washed it off up in our room. I suppose it seems obvious now but last night I was so upset I didn't stop to think. And now, my clothes are ruined as the wine stains won't come off… And that was a shalwar I wore for actual weddings!"

"Don't worry about that! I told you I'd buy you a new one…" Riaz said immediately.

This was a small room, and I realized the Malwattes too were listening to the story.

"Hi, Mr. and Mrs. Malwatte," I greeted them, "would you like to join us?"

We manoeuvred the chairs to form a circle of sorts.

"Did the police speak to you last night?" I asked Hamzah.

"No, we ordered room service and went to sleep."

"Then this may be a good chance to jog your memory. You'll be able to give a more accurate account when they question you today."

Hamzah looked startled.

"Oh, it's nothing to be worried about. We were all questioned last night. You're lucky you avoided that – it was past midnight when we finally made it up to our room," said Vino.

"Alright. What else might they ask?"

"They expected us to recall everything that we saw and heard from the moment we arrived," said Mrs. Malwatte with a sigh.

"Fortunately, we checked in after lunch yesterday, and rested in our room until it was time to gather at the rooftop."

"When did you arrive?" I asked Riaz.

"We got here just before noon. I remember saying it's a good thing the rooms were prepared because usually, in the big hotels, they make you wait until 2 p.m. to check in."

"And then?" I prompted.

"We had lunch and relaxed in our room. Then we came down to the pool. We saw you and the two young men." His lips twitched. "And then we went back up to get ready for the event."

"I think you were already at the rooftop when we got there," Vino commented.

"Yes, we were the first to arrive. We spoke to Mr. Peiris for a while and then mingled with the other guests until they kicked things off."

"Did you know anyone else participating in the event?"

"I'd met Mr. Peiris in Colombo," he said. "I'm also in the travel industry."

"Oh? Do you have a travel agency?" I asked.

"Yes. It's a small affair and we specialize in customized tours around the country for foreigners who like to experience something other than sun and sand."

We all smiled at that.

"We're checking out this, and a few other newer hotels in the area," he went on. "Places that can provide something different."

"Oh, yeah, this is as different as it can get!" muttered Hamzah.

"Do you know anything about Mr. Peiris?" I asked, keen to know something about our new boss. "I think he's quite brave to invest in a place in the middle of nowhere."

"He's actually got a good nose for business. Most Sri Lankan hotels are in either the cultural triangle or by the beach. But there are so many other opportunities. Take this area, for example. Yes, it's in the middle of nowhere, but it also provides a glance at authentic village life to visitors from more developed countries. Mr. Peiris said he's organizing immersive experiences with the villagers like cookery classes and bullock cart rides. That will be extremely popular if it is marketed well."

"You make quite a good sales pitch," I complimented him. "I'd book a tour with you if I were a traveller!"

"Yes," agreed Mr. Malwatte. "I have some friends visiting from overseas. Maybe I can pass on your details to them."

"Thank you so much. I appreciate that," said Riaz, eagerly reaching for his business cards.

I turned to Hamzah. "And what do you do?"

"I run my own business from home."

"That's interesting! Do you specialize in handmade products? Or are you a home cook? There are so many small businesses that function on social media now," I said.

"I make jewellery."

"Do you have a business card? My friends are always on the lookout for unique customized pieces. I can refer your work," offered Mrs. Malwatte.

"Thank you so much! No, I don't have any cards. Riaz keeps reminding me to print some. Shall I write my social media handles at the back of his card?" said Hamzah, blushing.

"Of course, dear. I'm happy to help."

I winked at Vino as they bent over the table. The Malwattes were taking the younger couple under their wing.

I cleared my throat. Time to get this discussion back on track.

"So, how did you all fare with the Murder Event?" I asked. "Were you able to figure out who killed the Bride?"

They all laughed.

"No. I think they should have allotted more time," said Mr. Malwatte. "And handed out notepads and pens! I just couldn't keep track of who said what. I didn't even get the opportunity to talk to everyone! What about you, dear?" he asked his wife.

She too shook her head. "Asking the correct questions was tougher than I anticipated," she said. "It made for some unusual conversations."

"Oh, yes," laughed Vino. "One moment you're talking about pets and then suddenly someone asks what kind of car you drive! It was rather disorienting!"

"Did any of you speak to Serena?" I asked, steering the conversation.

"Yes, the three girls came down with us in the lift," said Mrs. Malwatte.

"Was Serena okay at that point?"

"Well, I don't want to speak ill of the dead, but she downed an entire glass of wine in the lift and grabbed a cocktail off a passing tray as soon as we stepped onto the lawn." She paused. "At that rate, I'm not surprised if she was drunk before the night was over."

"The tox screen will tell us her blood alcohol level," said Mr. Malwatte.

"If she was not in her proper senses," mused Hamzah, "anyone could have lured her away into the dark…"

We all considered that for a while.

"Anyway, she should not have been drinking," she went on. "It's not ladylike, and it's unhealthy!"

There was an awkward moment following this pronouncement.

I cleared my throat again. "So, did any of you find those clues they told us about? I found two pieces of paper and I think Vino found two."

"I found three," said Riaz.

"We found three as well," said Mrs. Malwatte.

Hamzah just sniffed.

I turned to the Malwattes. "Where did you find your clues?"

"We didn't venture far. After the death note was read out, we checked the dining table, and the fence and bushes close by." Mrs. Malwatte laughed. "I think it was pure luck that we found three!"

"You know, I'm disappointed that they couldn't finish the game," confessed Vino. "I was really into it. I wanted to know who did it!"

"Maybe you can figure out who killed Serena, and that will make you feel better," said Hamzah.

"Yes, I just might do that." Vino did not get rattled often but I could tell that Hamzah's attitude was getting under her skin. She sounded exasperated.

"Anyway," I said, "About that. Did any of you see Serena move away from the pool?"

We all exchanged glances. No one replied.

"She was lying back in a deck chair while I was checking the umbrellas," said Riaz. "Then I moved off towards the changing rooms, and after that the dining table."

"There were a lot of people moving around. The guests. The wait staff. And although the lights were bright in the centre, there were pools of darkness everywhere. We may never know what happened," said Mr. Malwatte, sombrely.

Although I agreed with his evaluation of the evening, I did not believe that the murder would go unsolved.

"We can't let that happen. There were fourteen of us walking around! Someone must have seen something!" I insisted.

Mrs. Malwatte laid a well-manicured hand on my arm.

"Yes, dear. But do you know what scares me? There were so many of us up and about. Who commits murder in the midst of a crowd? Someone who is either brazen or desperate or both. They could have been seen at any time and it was probably pure luck that they managed to go unnoticed. I hope the police find out who it was, sooner than later."

"We can't wait for the police," I said. "Time is running out. If you remember anything, any tiny insignificant detail, please tell either me or Vino, or Mr. Peiris, or the cops themselves. We have to work together to solve this puzzle."

CHAPTER EIGHT

VINO LINKED HER arm through mine as we strolled about the lawn.

"I'm glad you made that speech back there, insisting that they share any information with us," she said, "but could it have painted a target on our foreheads?"

"What do you mean?"

"Everyone working together to solve the crime is commendable, but don't forget, one of them is a killer. If they realize that you're keen to find them, they may come after you next!"

I scoffed at the idea. "I highly doubt a serial killer is on the loose! Anyway, it's too late to worry about that now." I dragged her towards the trees to the left. "Let's visit the scene of the crime."

I had not explored this part of the garden during my previous visit to the hotel. There was an old-fashioned waist-high wooden fence with a swinging door, decorated by a green leafy vine with small white flowers, about twenty metres away from the pool. The lawn extended further past the fence. The gate was unlatched so we pushed it open. Larger trees like mango, jak, and kottamba provided a much welcome shade and a swing made of rope and a wooden plank hung from one of the thicker branches nearby. The grove was charming and imbued with an air of innocence.

"I wonder where they found her?" Vino whispered.

"There." I too kept my voice low as I pointed to a few mismatched stakes which had been used to cordon off a patch of earth by a metal bower.

My eyes filled and my throat tightened as I looked at the crooked sticks that marked the sad little space. I had not spoken kindly to Serena. I had felt irritated by her attitude and behaviour. But no one deserved to die like this. Alone. In the darkest corner.

Vino sniffed next to me, and I put an arm around her waist. She wiped away her tears and pointed to a small oil lamp which was barely visible in the grass.

"Someone cared."

I nodded. I couldn't trust my voice to speak.

I edged closer to the spot and squatted to take a closer look.

"What are you searching for?"

"The wine stain. Or shards of glass. Hamzah said a glass of wine must have spilled or broken. I can't see anything."

Vino joined me on the grass. "You know, all this time, while we were questioning everyone, it felt like part of the game. Just a puzzle that had to be solved." She gestured to the lamp. "This, this makes it so much more real. More human."

"More of a tragedy," I whispered.

"Yes."

We sat in silence.

I had not prayed for years. Although baptized as a Catholic at birth, I had not been to a church since my wedding. My heart clenched as I thought of Serena's last moments. Had she known what was happening? Or had she been too drunk to understand? Had she believed in the afterlife?

I repressed a shudder as morbid thoughts flooded my mind. Shaking my head to chase the shadows away, I rose and looked around. I found what I wanted in the far corner by the wall – an araliya tree in full bloom. Plucking some of the dainty fragrant magenta flowers I arranged them around the single lamp. Closing my eyes, I offered a simple prayer for Serena's soul.

When I was done, I walked past the stakes up to the far wall which marked the end of the property, scanning the surrounding area for any clues. A nondescript wooden door could be seen where the garden wall joined the building further down. Perhaps a service entrance.

Vino tugged at my hand. "The police have taken everything of importance into evidence. Let's go."

As we walked away, she added, "I feel sorry for Hamzah. We only saw the remnants of the scene and I have a headache. Just imagine what she went through last night!"

I made a beeline for a garden seat under a shady tree and took a deep calming breath. Exhaling, I dug into my handbag. "Right. Back to work. Let's add to our notes before we forget what was said in the library."

Vino sat back and muttered answers while I wrote down what we had learned so far. It was quiet and relaxing. The soft breeze playing on our faces and the bright sunshine were a significant change from the gloomy scene of Serena's demise. I felt the tension fade and I marvelled, as I often did since moving out of Colombo, at the tranquillity of rural life. The scorching midday heat had driven everyone else indoors. The murmur of voices and the chirping of birds in the trees were the only discernible sounds abroad. I considered taking a break too and retiring upstairs to our room for a short nap.

Clicking the notebook shut with a snap I said, "Let's go in. Keep an eye out for the Americans and the boys."

"Speak of the devil," muttered Vino as two familiar figures appeared around a bush.

"Kimaya! Vino! We haven't seen you since breakfast! Would you like to join us for a late lunch?"

It was Chris and Chamil.

"It's Kiyama, actually. We were just thinking of making our way in," I said, trying not to roll my eyes.

There was no buffet laid out for lunch, so Vino and I opted for soup and salad while Christ and Chamil chose sandwiches from the a' la carte menu.

"Not fond of rice?" I asked as the waiter took our orders.

"It's nice to have something different," Chamil responded. "Anyway, I try to stay away from heavy meals in the afternoons."

"You two must be on a diet. All women are on an eternal diet," laughed Chris.

I forced myself not to scowl at him. "No, actually we had a heavy breakfast and then coffee a short while ago so I'm just not very hungry."

"So, what do you do for a living?" Vino asked, changing the subject.

"I'm a personal trainer and I own a gym in Colombo," said Chamil.

"I'm an entrepreneur," said Chris.

"Specializing in?"

"Oh, anything that needs to be imported. I have a colleague in the US who coordinates at that end. Individuals order whatever they want delivered to his place and he loads it all into one container. Everyone splits the shipping cost. I clear everything at customs at this end. It's an import business, of sorts."

"Right," I said. His business sounded as dodgy as he did!

"What about you? What do you do?" Chamil asked.

"I own and run a rubber estate in Parkaduwa," said Vino. "And Kiyama is visiting me on holiday between jobs at the moment."

"Wow, a woman of leisure and pleasure, nice!" said Chris.

I winced.

"So, when did you two check in?" It was now my turn to change the subject.

"We arrived yesterday, before lunch. We didn't want to spend too much time here in the back of beyond," said Chris with a smirk.

"Why did you decide to participate in this event anyway if it's in the back of beyond?" I snapped.

"Hey, don't take it personally. I know you live here, but come on, don't you yearn for the sights and sounds of civilization?"

"We like it here fine. I'm a huge fan of crime fiction and that's why we bought tickets to this thing. How about you?"

"And why am I getting the third degree suddenly?" he retorted, defensively.

Oh-uh, that came out too strong.

"Sorry," I said, trying to sound as sincere as I could fake it. "Just keen to solve this mystery, since the event didn't end as expected."

"Hmpf, you could say that again," muttered Chris.

"So, Chamil, I am genuinely curious. Why did you guys participate in this event?" asked Vino with a winning smile.

"It was Chris's idea. He said he had someone to see in the area and this was the only decent hotel for miles. We thought we could do something fun during the trip."

"And you just tagged along…"

Chamil shrugged. "I needed a holiday."

"Okay…"

Vino and I exchanged glances. These two were hiding something.

"So, what did you do after breakfast today?" I asked, trying to lighten the mood.

"We had a swim mid-morning. Pity you weren't there," Chris sniggered.

I resisted the urge to kick him. If not for the investigation, I would have left the table by now. How could someone be so boorish? Was it all an act? Was he the killer hiding behind this offensive exterior? If only all dreams came true!

Sensing my mood Vino continued the conversation. "We went back up and checked in on Kumudu and Minosha."

"How are they holding up?" asked Chamil. He seemed sincere.

"Not too bad, considering. They just needed someone to talk to. We decided to ask around and see if any of the other guests heard or saw anything relevant yesterday."

"Isn't that the job of the police?" Chris asked.

"Yes, but it will give the girls a sense of closure. I think they feel responsible for not keeping an eye on Serena," I explained.

"That's ridiculous! The girl was drunk! She could barely stand straight!"

I looked at Chris in interest. "When did you notice that?"

"When we spoke to them by the pool. Her answers were incoherent nonsense! I don't think she was even following her character card. I remember wondering how many drinks she had had to behave like that!"

"Did you see her after the death notice was read? While we were all searching for clues?"

"I didn't go that way. I hunted among the bushes and pathways. But Chamil went towards the pool, didn't you?" said Chris.

We all looked towards him.

"Yes, both Riaz and I inspected the deck chairs and umbrellas for a while. She giggled and invited me to check under her chair, which I declined," he answered, flushing a little.

"You should have accepted the invitation mate!" said Chris with a coarse laugh. "Those legs and that dress…"

I cleared my throat. Such a pity it was not Chris who was strangled last night. The killer would have done the world a favour!

"Riaz moved off to the right and I searched those large pots at the entrance to the building," Chamil continued. "And then, I just walked around I think, I can't remember exactly where I went."

"Where were you when Hamzah ran in?" I asked.

"I was seated at the dining table, checking the centre arrangements," said Chamil.

"And where were you?" I asked Chris.

"Where was I when…?"

"When Hamzah ran in."

"Oh… erm… let me think… Wasn't I also at the dining table?" He looked quizzically at his friend.

"I… can't recall," said Chamil.

"Ah, yes, I received an important phone call, and I was in the bushes, talking!" said Chris with a big grin.

That sounded suspicious and rather convenient. Unfortunately, our discussion was cut short by the arrival of the food and although I attempted to steer the conversation back, both Chamil and Chris insisted on discussing mundane matters thereafter.

We would have to dig deeper to find out what was going on.

We excused ourselves as soon as we had finished the mains, declined dessert, and escaped to the lobby, only to walk slap bang into Inspector de Silva at the reception.

"Oh, hello Inspector!" I said cheerfully. "Back so soon?"

"Yes," he said drily, "we have a few more interviews to conduct. Sorting out the timelines of fifteen people is not easy."

"You can say that again," I muttered.

"Excuse me?"

Oops, I had not meant to say that out loud!

"No, nothing important! I was just sympathizing with your plight," I said quickly. "Anyway, got to go, we were on our way upstairs to rest."

I dragged Vino off towards the lift. She was stifling her laughter.

"What?"

"It's just that you behave very strangely whenever the good Inspector is around," she observed.

"It's just the way he looks at me. I automatically feel guilty even when I've done nothing wrong!"

"That must come in handy in his line of work."

"Yes, well, let's leave him to his work and get on with ours."

I stopped to let us into our room.

"We need to sort through everything we heard and make a timeline, like he said."

"We also need to speak to Megan and Rob," Vino pointed out. "I haven't seen them since breakfast. Maybe they stepped out to visit the village?"

"May be,"

We lapsed into a short silence as we each pondered our next move. I whipped out my notebook and entered the latest information.

"I have an idea!" I said, reaching for the phone. "Hello, is that the reception? This is Kiyama Fernando from Room 204. Can you please send up Siril? He brought our bags up for us yesterday. Thanks."

"What are you up to, Kiy?"

"We need someone who works here to tell us the latest gossip. We also need another set of eyes and ears. Siril is the best option. He knows who we are and how we were involved with the last investigation. He can help."

"You know, that's not a bad idea!"

My reply was cut off by a knock at the door. "Hello, Siril," I said, letting him in. "We need your help."

"Yes, Miss. Anything you want, Miss," he replied.

"Vino and I are looking into the murder of Serena Perera. Quietly, on the side, if you understand what I mean. Since you work here, we were wondering if you could tell us what you saw and heard yesterday. And anything you observed about the guests."

He looked at me sceptically. "I did not see anything odd, Miss."

"That's okay. To start off with, have you seen the two foreigners today, since breakfast?"

He frowned in thought. "I saw them in the front garden in the morning. They were getting into a trishaw."

"Did you see them return?"

"No. I have been helping to clear up the food and dishes in the dining area. Coming to think of it, I did not see them having lunch."

"That's very helpful, thanks. Now, do you remember seeing Serena, the girl who was killed, out and about yesterday and the day before?"

"Sorry, Miss. I honestly do not remember."

I bit my lip. This was harder than expected.

"What were your duties yesterday during the event?" Vino asked.

"I arranged the furniture both at the rooftop and in the lawn. Then once the guests moved downstairs, I cleaned up the rooftop area. After that I did not have any definite duties as such, so I hung around watching all of you talking and searching for clues.

Some of the other staff were also watching from inside the building."

"That's great!" I said. "That's just what we need. Someone who was observing rather than participating. Did you see anyone doing anything out of the ordinary?"

"What do you mean, Miss?"

"Like anyone watching Serena without participating in the event… or someone talking on the phone instead of looking for the hidden clues?"

"Ah, yes, now I remember! That short fat gentleman in glasses…"

"Chris David?"

"Yes, that is the name. He was on the phone, arguing like, while everyone else was searching for the slips of paper. I also saw him talking to Kapila, in a corner."

"Who's Kapila?"

"He's one of the kitchen staff. They don't usually come out during events because they are so busy preparing the food, but like I said, everyone was curious to see what was happening, you know, with Miss Lavanya pretending to be dead and all. So I was not that surprised to see him outside. I was surprised to see him talking to Mr. Chris, though."

"Did you hear what they were saying?"

"No. I was near the building, and they were in the garden. I saw Mr. Chris waving his arms around, like this." Siril raised both arms and gestured energetically like an actor from a bad tele-drama.

"That's very helpful, Siril," I praised him, feeling a surge of excitement. This should help us discover what Chris was hiding.

"Did you see Serena at the pool?"

"She ordered a *lot* of drinks," he said sheepishly. "Actually, some of us had a bet going to see how many glasses she would take."

"And how many did she have?" asked Vino, who had kept silent up to now.

"Four! And then she got up very unsteadily and walked off into the garden. I remember someone joking about how she might dive headfirst into the pool in those high heels!"

"She just got up and walked off?" I asked confused.

"Yes, I think she found a clue under her deck chair. So, she may have decided to participate in the game after all."

"Was she carrying a glass of wine with her when she walked off?" asked Vino.

"I think so... yes."

"Did you see where she went?"

"I watched her for a while, but she did not fall over. She just disappeared to the left."

"Wait, let me get this straight. You were standing at the main glass doors. The pool was in front of you, and further down, the garden where the dining area was set up. The changing rooms would be to your right."

I paused and he nodded.

"So, what's to the left? We walked that way today. There's just a smaller door to the building, the bower, and the bigger trees. Was that area lit up at all last night?"

"No. Mr. Peiris did not want anyone wandering off into that area so only the mood lighting under the trees were on."

"Well, that didn't stop Serena or Hamzah from walking into the area…Where does the door lead?"

"That is a service entrance. We use it to go in and out of our quarters and to access the kitchen."

He started to fidget. "Erm… Miss… if you do not have any real work for me… I can go back downstairs, no? I have dishes to clean and if I do not get that done soon I cannot take a break in the afternoon…"

I stood up and pressed some cash into his hand. "Thank you, Siril. That was extremely helpful. Please let us know if you recall anything else. Or see anything suspicious."

And as he turned to leave, I added, "By the way, don't tell any of the other staff we're asking questions. You know how Miss Vino and I like to solve puzzles… we're just being curious."

Vino let out an explosive sigh and fell back onto the bed.

"This is giving me a headache! So many suspects! And no one saw anything!"

CHAPTER NINE

I **SANK INTO** the soft bed and closed my eyes. Vino was not the only one with a headache. I would have to take two panadols before bedtime or I would not get any sleep.

"No," I disagreed, "we know quite a lot. But the information needs to be organized. Come on, you're the logical accountant here. Let's put your brain to work!"

I reached for my notebook. Flipping through it I said, "Let's make a list of observations and suspicions."

1. Kumudu seemed jealous of Serena's success
2. Serena had an argument with Megan at the bar – talk to the bartender

3. The girls didn't speak to anyone else before the event

4. The three girls were together throughout the event until the scavenger hunt

5. Riaz, Chamil, and Siril all saw Serena at the pool

6. She suddenly got up and walked off by herself

7. She carried a glass of wine. Wine was spilt by the body

8. Chris is on a shady business trip – talk to Kapila

I considered what I had put down. "What's your gut feeling about each of the guests, Vino?"

"Well... I don't think the Malwattes, Hamzah, or Riaz had anything to do with the murder. They all arrived on Saturday afternoon, kept to themselves, and attended the event. They were also clear about their movements while searching for clues. Chris, on the other hand, is our prime suspect, I think. We need to find out what he was doing during the scavenger hunt."

"Yes," I agreed. "Can you remember where everyone was when Hamzah ran in?"

"Let's see. I was by the bushes near the poruwa. You, Kumudu and Minosha were at the poruwa. Mr. Peiris and Lavanya were at the dining table throughout the hunt. The Malwattes said they stayed by the table too... Where were Chamil and Riaz?"

I flipped through my notes. "They were both near the pool and then at the dining table."

"Only Chris is unaccounted for," Vino noted with a grim smile. "We keep returning to him, don't we?"

"But we still don't know what the Americans were doing," I reminded her. "We didn't ask the others if they saw them during the hunt. We'll have to slip that into the conversation at some point."

The phone rang. Vino answered.

"What?" she said. "Wait. Slow down. What is missing? Stay there. We'll be right over."

I stood up. "Who was that?"

"Minosha. They were packing Serena's stuff. Apparently, the pendant she bought on Friday is missing."

We raced to Room 201 to find Kumudu and Minosha rummaging frantically through some makeup bags at the bathroom counter. They looked harassed.

"Are you absolutely sure Serena kept the pendant here?" I asked as we helped the girls organize the items.

"Positive," said Kumudu. "She wore it here saying the lighting is better than in the room. Then she put it into her pouch."

"And that was on…?" asked Vino.

"Friday evening."

"Did she wear it out after that?"

Kumudu looked at her friend. "Didn't she wear it down to dinner that night and to breakfast on Saturday morning?"

Minosha's eyes lit up. "Yes!" she exclaimed, "with that scoop necked turquoise top! The pendant was a beautiful greenish blue coloured stone set in silver and shaped like a large teardrop," she added for our benefit.

"So, anyone who was in the dining area at the time would have seen it," I said cautiously.

Minosha gasped. "Do you think one of the staff stole it?"

I preferred giving them the benefit of the doubt, so I said, "We don't know for sure. Did you see her return it to the pouch after breakfast?"

Kumudu's eyes lost focus as she considered this. Finally, she nodded. "Yes. We walked around the hotel and the grounds for a while and then came up. Serena changed into a t-shirt to relax, and I remember her saying that the chain was chafing a little."

I looked at the messy bedroom. "Have you checked everywhere? Are you sure it's missing? I mean it's small. It could have slipped into any nook or cranny."

"*Yes!*" Kumudu insisted. She gestured at the room. "This mess is because we searched everywhere! We shifted the mattress and checked between the cushions and under all the furniture! And now we have to put everything back!"

I let out a sigh. *This is all we need. Could this be connected to the murder?*

I checked my phone for the time. It was almost four o'clock.

"Vino, let's go and have a chat with Mr. Peiris. He needs to know about this."

"I hope Inspector de Silva is still here," I panted as we walked briskly down the corridor. "Missing jewellery is no laughing matter."

"Are we going to share everything we have learned with the police?" Vino asked.

I hesitated. While a part of me acknowledged the fact that withholding information was a bad idea, another part wanted to solve the puzzle first.

"Let's answer truthfully if asked, but not divulge anything voluntarily for now."

We inquired after Mr. Peiris who turned out to be in his private office with the police. The receptionist called ahead to warn them of our impending arrival.

"Come in, ladies!" he greeted us as we walked in.

The space was dominated by an impressive office desk which looked to be of real mahogany. The Inspector was seated in one of two traditionally carved straight back chairs opposite the owner of the hotel. A wall painting hung behind Mr. Peiris in keeping with the general theme of the hotel. Large standing lamps and a potted plant took up much of the remaining space.

The Inspector rose saying, "Please, take this seat."

An impromptu game of musical chairs was avoided by the inclusion of an extra chair from the lobby outside, and we finally got down to business.

"Mr. Peiris has informed me that you are also investigating this matter privately at his request," the Inspector said as soon as we were settled in.

"Yes."

"You look flustered. And the receptionist informed us that you have urgent news. Has anything happened?" Mr. Peiris interrupted leaning forward.

"Yes. Serena's two friends Kumudu and Minosha just informed us that a piece of jewellery has gone missing. It's a pendant Serena purchased from a gem museum on Friday. She wore it on Saturday morning. The girls were clearing up Serena's things when they realized it was gone."

"What?" exploded Mr. Peiris. "Are you accusing one of my staff of being a thief?"

"No!" I said, holding up my hand. "But it needs to be looked into, don't you think? The girls say they have searched the entire room, but it may be under the furniture, or the carpeting. We thought someone could assist them in cleaning up the place before questioning the staff."

"Yes…well, that's a good idea," muttered Mr. Peiris. He turned to the Inspector. "What would you suggest?"

"I can assign two policewomen to assist them. We need to check the victim's belongings anyway. And I will ask about it in the rest of my interviews with the staff."

Vino swivelled in her chair towards the Inspector and gave him a charming smile. "Have any test results come in yet? Like, do we know how and when she died?"

A smile tugged at the corners of the Inspector's mouth. He was amused!

"I would not normally reveal such information to civilians," he started, "but since Mr. Peiris has made a special request, I'll let you know this much. Yes, she was drunk when she was killed. Her blood alcohol level was high. She was not moved after death, so the scene of the crime is where she was found. She was strangled. Someone used their bare hands. As to when, we have witnesses who saw her walking towards that part of the garden. We think she was killed shortly before Ms. Hamzah stumbled across the body."

Vino's eyes were wide. I expected mine were too.

"Someone strangled her moments before Hamzah walked that way? So, where did he go?" I blurted out.

"It has to be a man, right?" Vino added, almost on top of me.

"Yes. The bruising on the throat indicates large hands so we are working on the assumption that it was a man. It does narrow the field down quite a bit."

"Someone from outside, dressed in white shirt and black trousers, would look like a waiter. He could just waltz in, do the deed and walk back out," observed Vino. "So, your field is not as narrow as you think!"

Inspector de Silva nodded. "We have taken that into consideration. If that were the case, then finding the killer is going to be near impossible. As far as we know, she knew no one in this area, so it is much more likely that the murderer is someone in this hotel."

We all sat in silence, letting that sink in. I swallowed hard. It was a dreadful thought. We may have shared a meal with a killer this weekend. Or we may have been served by one.

Mr. Peiris, who had been listening intently to this exchange, said, "Thank you, ladies, for informing us about the missing pendant. I'm sure we can handle that from our end. How are your interviews going?"

I shrugged noncommittally. "We've spoken casually to everyone except the Americans whom we didn't see around today. We're still trying to organize our notes. Give us a few hours to put some method to the madness and we'll share it."

"Megan and Rob hired a trishaw and driver today to visit Ratnapura. They should be back in time for dinner," Mr. Peiris said. "Is there anything else?"

Vino and I looked at each other. "No," we chorused. "Nothing important."

Vino and I decided to have a cup of coffee in the library while we perused my notebook and planned our next move. But first, leaving her to decipher my messy scrawl, I made a quick detour to the washrooms.

The nearest washrooms were the ones we had used during our disastrous visit a few months ago. Suppressing a shudder and telling myself not to be a goose, I turned in. One door led to the gents and the other to the ladies. I received a nasty shock while using the services when a loud bang emanated from the adjoining room. What on earth was going on in the gents' bathroom? Could someone have slipped and fallen?

I paused on my way out. I could not very well poke my head in to see if everything was alright, so I decided to eavesdrop at the door instead. A male voice could be heard clearly through the partition. It was Chris.

He sounded enraged. He was attempting to speak in a whisper, but his emotions were so high his voice was clearly audible. The rapid speech was interrupted by another bang as he kicked violently at something (probably a cubicle door).

"Now you listen to me you... I travelled all the way from Colombo to this hell hole to collect those packets. I *need* the shipment *tomorrow*. I have other business back home and I can't stay here any longer... What do you mean Mr. Ariyawansa doesn't have enough ganja?... You promised me the *excess* after selling to the Ayurveda shops! I have clients lined up waiting for this!... Urgh!"

This was followed by another slam.

I spun on my heels and made a quick getaway.

I was panting when I raced into the library and took refuge in an armchair.

"What on earth happened?" Vino gasped.

"Chris…" was all I could get out.

"Yes… What about him?"

"Shouting… in the bathroom…"

She looked confused. I held up a hand and gasped, "Give me a second."

I took a deep breath. "Chris was in the gents. I heard him on my way out. He was having a major argument with someone… They mentioned Ariyawansa."

Vino's eyebrows shot up in alarm.

"Apparently whoever he was arguing with had promised him some ganja but not delivered it. Chris was mad because he has customers waiting back in Colombo."

"And Ariyawansa is involved in this illegal cannabis trade?"

I recalled our last encounter with Ariyawansa with a shudder… The claustrophobic office… his oily confidence… the knowing looks… the note he had left at our house… "I'm not the least bit surprised," I sniffed. "I can't easily forget that dingy gambling den. I'm sure there's more than booze consumed there!"

"Well, I remember the mysterious message he sent us about owing him a favour. That gave me nightmares for a few days!" said Vino.

"So, Chris is involved in drug smuggling. He must have a contact here in the hotel. Remember how he was seen arguing with that guy – what was his name?"

"Kapila," supplied Vino.

"Yes! What if Serena heard them arguing? Or, how about this, if he has clientele in Colombo, she could very well be buying from him! Maybe she had a drug habit!"

"Woah, back up a second," Vino said. "It can't be both of that. If she was a customer, then she knew about the illegal drugs and there was no need to silence her."

That did not dampen my enthusiasm. "See, you're the logical one! So, she didn't do drugs. She just stumbled onto them!"

"It's definitely a possibility." She stood up. "Come on, we need to catch Inspector de Silva before he leaves. We can't keep this to ourselves."

The policeman had already left by the time we reached the reception desk, but the Americans were just entering the premises. We hung around so that we could bump into them 'accidentally-on-purpose.'

"Megan! Rob!" Vino cried in faux surprise. "Hi! Remember us? I'm Vino. This is Kiyama. Have you been evading the police?"

"No… we spoke to them last night," Rob replied in his Southern drawl.

"Well, you missed round two. They just left. Have you been out on a private tour?"

"Yes!" exclaimed Megan excitedly. "And look!"

She held up her left hand. A beautifully crafted blue sapphire ring adorned her fourth finger. "We're officially engaged!"

"Wow! Congratulations! Come on, let's sit somewhere so that you can share all the details!" Vino replied enthusiastically.

For someone who is resolutely single, she is a hopeless romantic at heart. Vino dragged an all-too-willing Megan out to the pool side while I exchanged a look with Rob and shrugged.

"Can't defeat them, join them?" I suggested.

Megan was in full flow when we each perched on the edge of our respective deck chairs. "I thought we were sightseeing. Then the driver took us to this really amazing gem museum. The jewellery was breath-taking! I should have been suspicious because Rob kept lagging behind. Then, just before we left, he produced *this!*"

"Did you go down on one knee?" Vino asked Rob with a wink.

"Of course he did!" Megan squealed as she threw her arms around him and kissed him thoroughly.

I couldn't help smiling in turn. Her excitement was infectious.

"Well, we're still two weddings short," I said. Seeing their blank faces, I added, *"Four Weddings and a Funeral.* Don't tell me you haven't heard of it! It's a classic RomCom!"

Vino laughed. "These two would have been in diapers in the early 1990s Kiy!"

I waved that comment away. "Details!"

Megan clapped her hands. "I *love* romantic comedies. I'll make sure to check it out."

"It's British," I warned.

"So," said Rob, changing the subject, "any news on the murder?"

"We were curious, so we spoke to all the other guests. Everyone else stayed in-house today, by the way. A few people saw Serena walking off towards the side garden but that's it. Did you see anything suspicious last night? Can you take us through what happened from the time you checked in?"

Rob looked surprised, so I explained. "Minosha and Kumudu told us you were already here on Friday when they checked in. Did you see Serena around? Did she do anything suspicious? Maybe talk to any of the hotel staff or anyone from outside?"

"We've already spoken to the cops."

"Yes… but, you know how these rural police forces can be," I said, apologizing to Inspector de Silva in my head, "if we want to know what happened before we all leave tomorrow, we'll have to figure it out for ourselves!"

Megan twiddled with her new ring, while Rob looked out over the green landscape. It was dusk. I realized with a jolt that I was escaping from Chris's unwanted attentions a mere 24 hours ago. It felt like a lifetime.

"Let's see if I can remember my movements at the event yesterday," he said finally. "We got to the cocktail party quite early. Riaz and his wife were there talking to the owner of the hotel. Then once we came down here, we mingled with everyone." He looked at me. "We spoke to you for a short time, remember?"

"Yes."

"I don't think I spoke to you, Vino," he continued. "The murder mystery event was a good idea. But they didn't give us enough time."

"Do you recall what happened after you read the death note?" I inquired.

"Megan walked off to search for clues. I stayed where I was near the table and watched everyone scurrying around for a while. Then… I searched the bushes."

"Did either of you go into that garden area beyond the quaint fence?" I asked, pointing. "We explored that today. To be honest, I didn't even see it in the dark last night!"

Megan squirmed a little in her seat and said, "Yes. I walked that way but soon returned when I realized it was badly lit and we were not meant to be there."

"Oh?" I said, curious. "Did someone tell you it's out of bounds?"

"Yes. I met a guy from the hotel staff. He was taking a smoke break and seemed surprised to see me wandering about. He pointed me in the direction of these deck chairs and said, confidentially, that he had seen the girl who played the Bride messing with them. So, I came this way."

I bit my lip in excitement. No one else had mentioned this!

I caught Vino's eye. "What did the smoker look like?" she asked, attempting to sound calm.

Megan shrugged. "He was dressed in one of those uniforms kitchen staff wear."

"Do you recall where you were, and who was nearby when Hamzah ran in?"

They both paused to think.

"I was near the changing rooms," Rob told us. "I remember spinning around at her scream and she came running out of the gloom straight towards me." He rose and demonstrated as he spoke.

Megan giggled nervously. "I almost had a heart attack when she screamed like that! I was by these deck chairs, actually, taking a break."

I nodded. Now to the hard part. "Rob, did Serena recommend that gem museum by any chance, the one you visited today?"

Megan stiffened and glared at her fiancé.

"Well?" she snapped. "Did she?

Rob was looking uncomfortable. He messed with the hair at the nape of his neck and said, "So, what if she did? She said she bought a beautiful pendant there…"

Megan looked livid. She jumped to her feet and waved her beringed hand at us. "So, this ring is courtesy of that whore?" She yanked it off her finger and thrust it at me. "Here! Give it back to him!" Then, she pushed past us and raced back into the hotel.

Vino and I looked at Rob. He buried his face in his hands, looking devastated.

I silently held out the piece of jewellery which sparkled in the floodlights. "At least she didn't throw it into the pool."

Vino stifled a giggle.

Rob rewarded my effort with a watery smile. "Yes. It cost a fortune. And she is worth every dollar."

"If you don't mind me asking," said Vino. "Why is she so mad?"

"Because Serena was all over me at the bar on Friday night," Rob sighed. "She slipped me a note asking me to meet her in the library on the first floor that night. I threw it into the trash can in our room. Megan found it."

I winced. That would not have been pretty.

"Did you go?" Vino asked.

"Of course not!" he scoffed. "I didn't want to damage my relationship with Megan! I spent months organising this vacation. I had already decided to propose to her, and I wanted it to be memorable and romantic. An island paradise seemed just the place. I knew Ratnapura is famous for its gem industry, and I checked a few places online. A Ceylon blue sapphire… I knew what I wanted. I just hadn't sorted out the details."

"And Serena suggested a gem museum from which to buy the engagement ring?" asked Vino, perplexed.

"No! She just mentioned the name of the joint while showing off her new accessory and I Googled it later." He sighed again. "I've botched it, haven't I?"

"No, of course not" I said gently. "Take it from someone who's officially separated after years of marriage. This is a minor misunderstanding. Give her time to cool down and then give her the ring again and apologize."

"Grovel," suggested Vino. "Place the ring in some flowers, hide it in her drink or something romantic like that. Google it."

Rob pocketed the ring, stood up and held out his hand to me. "Thank you for your advice," he said as we shook. "I'll do that."

Vino and I watched as he walked purposefully back to the building.

"Well, that was eventful," I commented.

"And informative," she added.

"I wonder if Serena idled in the library for a while waiting for him to turn up?"

"Minosha and Kumudu insisted that nothing else happened on Friday night and that they went straight to bed," Vino noted.

"Perhaps Serena sneaked out and they didn't even know."

"Hmm… At least he was honest with us. When do you think he will realise that his story points the finger straight at Megan as a prime suspect?" Vino asked.

"He's troubled right now. It's a good thing he didn't think it through, or he would have lied."

She nodded. "So, what next?"

I reached into my handbag and dragged out my trusty notebook. "We don't need to talk to the bartender right now," I remarked. "We need to talk to Kapila. And we should try to catch Minosha by herself. I want to ask her about the friendship between Kumudu and Serena. Kumudu seemed rather bitter during our interview."

"Yes," Vino agreed. "I sensed that as well." She checked her wristwatch. "It's almost seven o'clock. Let's go up and change. Who knows, Rob might take my advice and propose to Megan over dinner!"

CHAPTER TEN

DINNER WAS CALM and uneventful. All the guests were present, except the Americans who had opted to order room service. The food, as before, was exceptional. I wondered where Mr. Peiris had found such an accomplished chef.

Towards the end of the meal, I spotted Minosha leaving the room by herself and followed her to the washrooms just outside.

"Minosha! Wait up. I want to ask you something."

She glanced up and down the corridor nervously and led the way in.

"I really have to go," she said, rushing into a cubicle.

I washed my hands for a while and adjusted my hair, waiting for her to come out.

"Minosha, I wanted to ask you something about Serena," I said when she finally joined me at the washbasins.

"But why did you have to sneak in here?"

"It's not sneaking. It's catching you by yourself. Kumudu has a strong personality and I wanted to hear you for a change," I said.

Minosha did not respond. But I knew she was listening.

I decided to put her at ease first. "Inspector de Silva mentioned that two policewomen would search through Serena's things for evidence. I hope they didn't disturb you too much."

"Oh no." She gave a small smile. "They actually helped us to clean up and even offered to keep an eye out for the missing pendant."

"Did they find it?"

"No." Her shoulders sagged.

"They're also interviewing the staff. I'm sure it will turn up," I said sympathetically. "So," I continued, moving on to what was foremost on my mind, "can you tell me what the friction was between Kumudu and Serena?"

She looked up like a frightened deer. "How did you know?"

"It doesn't take a genius to sense the undercurrent. Is she just angry that Serena was offered a top post in her father's company on a platter while she had to work hard to achieve her dreams? Don't get me wrong, I sympathize. Everything I have, I worked hard for, so I'd probably feel the same."

"Yes…"

"And…"

"And there was the thing about Lal…" She stopped.

I realized immediately where she was going with this. "Did Serena steal Kumudu's boyfriend?"

"He wasn't her boyfriend. Not officially, anyway. But they were dating. And then suddenly they weren't, and he was hanging out with Serena. That didn't last either." She shut the water off. "I personally think Kumudu dodged a bullet there. If he was ready to dump her and move on so fast, then it wouldn't have worked in the long term anyway."

Minosha was more astute than she appeared.

"Did you tell her that?" I asked.

"No! Of course not! I keep my opinions to myself!" She looked at me in alarm. "But I know Kumudu didn't kill her for it. That happened months ago, and anyway, Kumudu was with me the entire evening."

"Alright," I said, moving on. "Did Serena leave the room late on Friday night?"

Minosha's eyes widened. "How do you know *that*?" she whispered.

"Robert told us about the note. But he didn't show up for the tete-a-tete. So, Serena must have hung around in the library and then sneaked back in. Did you see her?"

"No, but…"

"Minosha," I said looking at her in the mirror. "I'm not the police. I won't pass on anything confidential that has no bearing on the murder. You can trust me. What did you see?"

"It's not something I saw. Felt, is more like it. Serena was in the single bed on the side. Kumudu and I shared the double. I felt Kumudu leave. I thought she was using the loo, but she opened the main door and left. When I looked around, I noticed that Serena's bed was also empty. I stayed awake, under the covers, until they both returned. First Serena and then Kumudu. Serena didn't check our side of the room, so she didn't know she was followed. She just slipped back into bed. I pretended to be asleep so neither of them realized I knew."

"Did you ask Kumudu about it the next day?"

"Yes. She told me what you just said. That Serena hung around and came back up. She had looked put out by something.

Kumudu assumed the same as you did, that Rob had stood her up."

She grabbed my hand. "Please," she said, "don't tell Kumudu I said any of this!"

Then she ran out.

Back in our room after dinner, I filled Vino in on what I had learned. She too was unsurprised to learn of the history between the girls.

"None of that proves that Kumudu is the killer," she observed.

"Yes," I agreed. "That leaves us with Megan, Chris, and Kapila."

"Right," she said, business-like. "Means, motive, and opportunity. Remember? Let's take them one by one. Megan."

"She definitely had motive, although if girls killed each other every time a man strayed, there'd be no women left!" I said, wryly.

Vino smiled. She knew my history with men going astray.

"Opportunity?" she prompted.

"She confessed to being in that part of the garden, so she had the opportunity. We really need to find the staff member who spoke to her. He may know what time it was since he was on a timed break, and whether she left after speaking to him, as she claimed."

"Means?

"She's about five feet six inches in height. And she hasn't got well-toned muscles or anything. I highly doubt she has the handspan or the strength to strangle Serena to death," I said thoughtfully.

"Also, given their history, Serena would not have allowed her to approach," Vino noted.

I scratched the name out.

We were down to two.

"Chris," I said.

"If Serena was not an existing client and she stumbled onto a drug deal, then he may have done away with her."

"He had the opportunity too," I said, "since he was not participating in the scavenger hunt but skulking among the trees instead."

"He isn't as buff as Chamil, but as you heard in the washrooms, he has a nasty temper and I'm sure he's quite capable of strangling someone in the heat of the moment."

"Okay. He stays on the list," I said. "And that leaves us with Kapila, who we know nothing about."

"He's the key to this puzzle," Vino said, gathering her night clothes, and heading for the bathroom to change. "Let's hire our friend Siril tomorrow as an assistant and sort this out once and for all!"

I arose early the next day, my overactive mind having kept me awake with arguments and counterarguments buzzing through my head. Since Vino too was up and about, we decided to head to the pool for an early pre-breakfast swim. The water was bracing, just what I needed to lift the cobwebs in my mind. After a quick breakfast we requested the reception to send Siril up to meet us as soon as his morning chores were complete. It was nearly 10 a.m. when he finally arrived.

"I am so very sorry to keep you waiting, Miss," he apologized as soon as he stepped in. "But I had a lot of work clearing up the breakfast room. So many plates!"

"That's okay, Siril," I said, setting him at ease. "We'll be leaving after lunch today. We'd like to speak to Kapila before we go."

"Kapila?"

"You said he was talking to Chris David on Saturday night during the event?"

"Ah, yes…" he looked down and shuffled his feet. "About that, Miss… I may have been mistaken…"

"What?" Vino and I both asked in surprise.

"It was dark… it was someone in kitchen uniform… I did not see the face clearly…" Siril stammered, wringing his hands.

I narrowed my eyes. "Siril," I said firmly, "has someone asked you to deny your previous statement?"

He fidgeted but did not answer.

"Is it Ariyawansa again?" Vino asked. "Has he threatened you?"

Siril's head snapped back up in shock. "No, Miss! None of this has anything to do with Ariyawansa!" He fiddled with the door, unable to open the simple mechanism in his haste. "I have work to do, Miss. Very sorry, Miss," he gasped as he bolted.

"The man doth protest too much," I said, turning to Vino.

She rose from her chair and marched to the door. "We don't need him, do we? We can ask Mr. Peiris to set up an interview. I actually felt sorry for him. We don't want to put him in hot water. Or put his mother in any danger from drug lords," she added. "We have to solve this soon and with minimum damage." She turned at the door. "We need to share everything we know with the police."

As per our request we were soon joined by Inspector de Silva and Mr. Peiris in the study.

"Have you solved the case?" asked Mr. Peiris hopefully, as the Inspector watched.

"Not fully," I said with a smile. I handed them each a sheet of paper with our observations. "We spoke to all the guests in turn and their movements are plotted on the map. I am sure Inspector de Silva too has reached the same conclusions. Of the fifteen people participating in the murder mystery only one person, Chris David, has means, motive, and opportunity."

Inspector de Silva glanced through the paper in his hand. "What motive would he have to kill Serena?"

"I overheard him arguing over the phone with someone about a shipment of ganja," I said succinctly. "You too may have discovered that he was seen in a heated discussion with a member of the kitchen staff. If they were talking about drugs and Serena overheard, he may have killed her to silence her."

Mr. Peiris stared at us, aghast. "Drug deals? In my hotel?"

Inspector de Silva showed no emotion but steepled his fingers before him and said, "We are aware of illicit drug trafficking in the area. Legally grown crops are used as a front. Ayurveda practitioners are legally permitted to use certain parts of the cannabis plant in their medications. The drug dealers use the excess stock to earn easy cash on the side. That is what Mr. David was hoping to take back with him to Colombo."

He rose. "Thank you, ladies. You have provided us with valuable information. We will take him and his friend into custody and interview them further."

"His friend?" Vino said.

"Yes. Chamil Hewage owns a string of gyms in Colombo, and it is possible that they are used to distribute the drugs."

"Please, Inspector, will you let us know the outcome?" I asked.

"Of course," he said as he exited the room.

"Then the case is solved and there is no need to detain the guests further. They can start checking out," celebrated Mr. Peiris happily, reaching for his phone.

"Wait. There is something else," I said. I had almost forgotten Kapila in all the excitement. "Mr. Peiris, do you have a man named Kapila working in the kitchens?"

'Perhaps," he said with a frown. "I don't know the names of all my staff. Why?"

"His name kept popping up. He may be Chris's contact in the drug deal. One person who wishes to remain anonymous told us he was the person arguing with Chris in the dark that night. Then

Megan told us a member of the kitchen staff spoke to her in the fenced garden area before the murder. We need to speak to him."

He jumped to his feet. "We need to call the police back!"

"No, wait, Mr. Peiris. Let us talk to him first while the police take in Chris and Chamil. A feminine touch may get more information out of him, don't you think?"

"Okay," he said, grudgingly. "But I will keep the police informed." He called the reception and asked them if Kapila was available.

"Kapila will be sent to you in the library," he told us as he hung up.

We rose. "Thank you, Mr. Peiris. We will let you know if anything else turns up."

Our plans were disrupted however, as we stepped into the lobby, by the sight of Chamil and Chris being escorted out of the hotel by the police. They were not in handcuffs, but the situation was obvious to all onlookers. And they had an audience. Everyone on the ground floor observed through the French windows or peeked around doors. A rustle of urgent whispers and the flash of phone cameras punctuated the silence.

Chris was almost purple with rage. "Don't you know who I am? I work closely with some prominent personalities! You won't have a job to go to in a few days!"

Vino and I stopped dead in our tracks, but Chris caught the movement out of the corner of his eye.

"I hope you two are happy," he spat. He advanced aggressively towards us but was blocked by a burly policeman. "This is *your* work, isn't it? Snooping around, sticking your noses where they are not wanted." He cackled coarsely and made a rude gesture. "Have you also been sticking your fingers in where they should not be?"

My heart hammered as he leered at us menacingly. I couldn't breathe. Vino too was immobile by my side.

He raised his voice so that he could be heard clearly throughout the building. "All of you enjoying the show, let me introduce you to two of our main performers today. Kiyama and Vino. Do you know what they are? Huh? Hiding behind this outer pretence of respectability. They're a pair of lesos! Lesbians! Man-haters! I figured it out when I saw them entwined in the swimming pool that first day! You couldn't deal with me face to face, so you ran to the cops with a tall tale! Huh!"

He was almost frothing at the mouth. Inspector de Silva put an end to his tirade by standing nose to nose and asking in a level voice, "Do you want me to add 'disturbing the peace' to your list of offences?"

"Homosexuality is also illegal, isn't it?" Chris retorted before clamping his mouth shut. His fists were still clenched though, and he was panting hard.

I glanced about wildly. Those standing closest to us had inched back creating an invisible wall around us. My eyes met those of Chamil who was standing silently behind Chris with a restraining arm on his friend's elbow. Chamil's eyes were cold and hard. We would find no sympathy there.

The quiet ones are sometimes more dangerous. Vino trusted you with her secret. How could you!

I swallowed hard. I tried to think of a clever comeback, but my mind was blank. Vino stirred next to me. I had forgotten, in my panic, that unlike me she really *was* a lesbian, and she must have heard such venom spewed at her many times before. Head held high she stepped up to the group huddled together by the door. When she spoke, her voice was even and emotionless. "Misogynistic asshole."

A few people tittered nervously. Soon, a gale of laughter flowed through the lobby.

Inspector de Silva gave us a nod and led Chris and Chamil out.

"Show's over folks. Don't you all have something else to do?" I muttered as I followed Vino's calm and confident stride through the gathered crowd towards the library. Although my eyes were fixed to the floor, I was aware of the sniggers and mutters that followed our path.

"I'm sorry you had to go through that, Kiy," she said softly as we settled into the armchairs by a window.

"You have nothing to be sorry about!" I burst out. "He's a vile, foul-mouthed… donkey!"

I started to laugh as I remembered the look on his face as he was finally led out. Vino soon joined me. The laughter did us good and I felt more relaxed afterwards.

"Your comeback was perfect," I said as I wiped tears off my cheeks. "My mind just froze, but you were so held together."

"I'm used to it," she said simply.

A wave of sorrow hit me as I watched my best friend. *Was prejudice and discrimination so common that she accepted it as another fact of life?* I reached over and squeezed her hand.

"Erm… Kiy," she said, not meeting my eyes, "Do you want to find another place to stay now?" Seeing the shock on my face she rattled on. "I mean, now that you've been associated with me in that way, and it's not even true in your case… I thought that you'd want to move out…"

"Vino!" I said. "Don't let that idiot's words get to you. I am not ashamed of sharing a house with you as a friend. Just as I know you're not ashamed of who you are. Kudos to you for believing in yourself and standing up to such shit. And I'm ready to stand by you. And I'm so sorry about Chamil. It looks like he did share your secret with Chris, in the end."

She nodded, her eyes glistening with tears.

Our quiet heart-to-heart was brought to an abrupt halt by a knock at the door. A young man dressed in the white uniform of the hotel kitchen staff stood there, peering in. Short, skinny, and sunburned to a dark brown, he looked more like a schoolboy playing truant than a member of the workforce. His clothes hung on him as if made to fit another.

"Good morning…. I was asked to speak to Miss Kiyama… and Miss Vinodhini?" he said timidly when he saw us.

"Ah, yes. Kapila, right?" said Vino, donning her most winning smile.

"Yes, Miss. I was told to meet you here."

"Kapila, shouldn't you be in school?" I asked, unable to contain my curiosity.

He grinned displaying a set of crooked teeth. "I just finished my O'Levels, Miss and I decided it was time to earn some money."

"You don't want to pursue your studies?"

A shadow flashed across his face as he looked down. "No, Miss. Sometimes we cannot have what we want."

"Do you live in Parkaduwa?" Vino asked.

"Yes. With my mother and younger sister."

As a former teacher my heart went out to this young man who wished to continue learning but was apparently unable to do so due to restrained circumstances and family commitments.

"Kapila," I said gently, "We need your help to corroborate some information. We heard that you took a smoke break on Saturday night and saw the foreign lady, Megan, in the side garden."

He looked as if he might bolt, so I quickly added, "Don't be alarmed! We aren't accusing you of anything. We just want to know if she was telling the truth… Did you see her and give her a tip to look by the pool during the scavenger hunt?"

He calmed down a little and nodded.

"Did you see anyone else in that area just before or after that?"

He shook his head mutely.

"Not even Mr. Chris?"

His eyes widened and his body involuntarily jerked back as if to fly. I forced myself to stay seated so as not to alarm him further.

Vino cut in softly. "Kapila, listen to me. The police have taken Chris and Chamil in for questioning. And they deserve whatever punishment they get. But we want to help you. Are you in any trouble? Did you agree to carry any messages or parcels for anyone?"

His prominent Adam's apple bobbed as he swallowed hard. "I was asked to deliver a message to Mr. Chris."

"Do you know what it said?"

"No. It was in a sealed envelope. But after reading it Mr. Chris started yelling at me saying this is not good enough and he wants the stuff immediately. I did not know what he was on about! When I told him I was only the messenger, he slapped me."

I winced as his hand strayed to his cheek and hoped Inspector de Silva threw the book at that good-for-nothing lout!

Scooting up to the edge of the chair I said, "Okay. We're not going to ask you who the message was from. But tell us this – did you see or hear anything suspicious that night? You were one of the few people in that part of the garden at that time. If you know anything, however insignificant it may seem, please share it with us. We can pass it on to the police."

He stiffened at the mention of the authorities.

"We will try our level best to prevent you getting embroiled in this any further. But you must stay away from Ariyawansa and his minions, however easy that money may seem. Can you do that?"

I saw him stiffen at the mention of Ariyawansa's name.

"I know nothing about Ariyawansa, Miss, or any of his business!"

"Kapila," I said, slowly and as evenly as I could. "Chris was in contact with Ariyawansa. You handed him a letter. It doesn't take a genius to put two and two together… And we don't care how or why you got involved… Okay? But I can give you one piece of advice: if you want to pursue a career and look after your family, you can't do that from inside a jail cell. Don't have anything more to do with you-know-who."

"Okay."

"I have a question," said Vino who had been observing quietly. "How often do the kitchen staff get a smoke break? Did you see anyone else go out after you?"

Kapila squirmed a little and said, "I did not actually get permission to step out. We are supposed to ask Mr. Rohan the Head Chef if we need any short breaks while we are on duty. I needed to pass on the message, so I sneaked out." He paused as if wanting to add something more but held his silence.

"Using the back door which connects to the garden?"

"Yes. Only us kitchen staff use that."

"Have any of your fellow workers been acting differently these past few days? Or has anyone mentioned anything odd?"

He fidgeted where he stood. Realizing he knew something, I said, "Kapila, we can't shield you from the police if you're hiding something."

He gulped and said in a rush, "My roommate on Saturday night – we share a dorm when we work late instead of going home – Pragath, he is a waiter, he served the drinks to the guests at the event, he said…"

"What did he say?" I asked, trying to stay calm.

"He said the bartender gave him a note with one of the drinks to be delivered to the girl who was killed!"

CHAPTER ELEVEN

AFTER THANKING KAPILA for confiding in us and instructing him to speak to us again if anything else came to mind, Vino and I raced to the bar which was set up by the French windows that lead out to the lawn and the pool.

It was empty.

Spotting Siril mopping the wet tiles outside Vino asked him to find the bartender saying we would like to enjoy an aperitif before lunch.

"If Serena received a note asking her to meet someone in the garden, then where's the note?" I pondered aloud as we waited.

"The Inspector didn't mention finding it so either the killer took it after the deed, or it was on the floor and got cleaned up with the rest of the litter after the event," Vino speculated.

"I just hope this guy can tell us who sent the note. That would make life so simple!" I said with a sigh.

Vino laughed. "Life is never simple!"

We were soon joined by a young fellow wearing a ponytail and a pleasant smile. His name tag read NALIN.

"Good afternoon, ladies! I am so sorry to keep you waiting, but I took a stroll outside since no customers were around. What can I get you?"

"Do you have a dry sherry or a light, white wine?" Vino inquired.

"Have you worked as a bartender for long?" I asked, to make conversation while he prepared our drinks.

"Oh, yes Miss! I worked at a few hotels around the island. But when I heard this place was opening and they had a vacancy, well, there's nothing like working near your own home, no?"

We chatted briefly about favourite beverages before guiding the conversation towards the night of the Murder Mystery Event.

"How did you manage by yourself during the event?" Vino asked. "I remember the waiters were being run off their feet with the drinks orders. And everything was so smoothly handled too."

"Some of the kitchen staff assisted me. You know getting the bottles down, washing the glasses, mopping up the spills, that sort of thing."

"I guess it helped that most of us were having wine rather than cocktails, huh?"

"Yes, Miss, definitely." He dropped his voice and leaned closer over the bar counter. "That girl who died ordered most of the cocktails. We almost kept a waiter to serve her exclusively!"

We smiled politely at what was obviously meant to be a witty joke.

I decided to take a shot in the dark. "Did anyone ask you to send a note to Serena, the girl who was killed?" I waved a hand. "We heard someone mention it."

"Oh that! I remember that note. It was under a glass I had prepared for her, and it had her name on it, so I sent it across." He winked. "I've seen all sorts of transactions happen under the influence. I thought someone was inviting her over for some fun later that night, you know." He stopped to consider this and grimaced. "Poor girl won't be enjoying anything now."

"Did you read it?"

"Of course not! That's a big no-no in this business!"

"Did you tell the police about the note?" I asked.

"Actually, Miss, I didn't. I had clean forgotten all about it until you asked me just now!"

"That's alright. Let's put our heads together and see if you can recall who else was here that night. We can then call the police on your behalf and give them the list of potential suspects." It was now my turn to drop my voice conspiratorially. "We're really curious to know who killed that girl."

"But didn't they arrest those two gentlemen?" he asked, looking confused.

"Yes. But that note is simply weird, don't you think? And I'm sure the police won't like any loose ends either. Okay. Let's start there. Did either Chris or Chamil approach the bar that night?" Vino asked.

He shook his head. "No. None of the guests came this way. You were all engrossed in the event."

Vino and I shared a startled look. That meant someone working at the hotel had left the note. But who?

"Do you remember who helped you here that night?" Vino asked, hopefully.

The bartender frowned in concentration. I crossed my fingers in my lap. "There were two boys from the kitchen assigned to the bar that day. Hasitha and Saman. Oh, and Head Chef Rohan was here for a while. He used to tend bars when he first started off in

Dubai. Man, he's still got a deft touch. He even helped me fix some of the drinks!"

"You're absolutely certain no one else came this way?" I persisted.

Nalin nodded. "But none of them would send a note to a guest, right? Someone must have put them up to it."

"Yes," Vino agreed thoughtfully. Then pretending to let the whole thing go, she added, "Oh well! There goes our chance at being super sleuths! Let's just forget about the note and enjoy our drinks!"

I checked my phone as we returned to the reception desk. "It's noon" I whispered. "Everyone will be checking out after lunch. We're running out of time."

"Well, if Chris is the killer, then this little discrepancy with the note may not be significant," Vino said. "But we should still inform the police, don't you think?"

I dialled the Eheliya police station on my mobile, but Inspector de Silva was unavailable.

"Probably questioning Chris and Chamil," I said after leaving a message and hanging up.

Our investigation hit a snag when the receptionist informed us that both kitchen workers Hasitha and Saman were on sick leave.

"I guess that leaves just the Head Chef," I told Vino. "We can't request that he meets us in the library. It's lunch time. We'll have to speak to him in the kitchen. Maybe he has an office in that area?"

It was not a good time to visit the kitchens. Servers moved in and out of the swinging wooden doors, platters in hand. We almost bumped into a trolley full of cutlery as we tried to catch someone's attention. Finally, I stopped a waiter who was clearing an empty table and asked, "Can we speak to Head Chef Rohan? Mr. Peiris sent us. It's kind of urgent."

"Now?" gasped the unlucky fellow. "He'll bite my head off if I disturb him now!" Then remembering his place, he ducked his head and muttered, "I'll see what I can do. Please wait here."

My stomach growled as we kicked our feet reminding me that I hadn't even had a snack since our early breakfast.

"You know, we have another unexplained lead," I said as I watched Mr. and Mrs. Malwatte, Riaz and Hamzah enter the hall together and serve from the buffet tables. "The pendant. How does that fit in with Chris's drug operation? It would make sense if someone killed Serena for her pendant but that's not what happened. Why would Chris need a piece of jewellery?"

Vino frowned. "Perhaps that's not a part of this? Maybe a member of staff did take it after Serena's death. Crime of opportunity?"

"Hmm…" I said, unconvinced.

Vino checked her wristwatch and whispered, "We've been standing here for almost fifteen minutes!"

My answer was cut short by the Head Chef's arrival. He looked harried and disgruntled. "Couldn't you have selected a more convenient time? We're in the middle of food service."

"We're truly sorry to disturb you, but you run a tight ship and I'm sure your staff can manage without you for a few minutes," Vino said. "I'm Vino and this is Kiyama. It's an honour to meet you in person – we've been raving about your food for the past two days!"

He looked a little less likely to chase us away, so I added, "We just have one small question about the time you spent helping out at the bar on Saturday…"

He wiped his hands on a serviette, returned it to the large pocket in his apron and sighed. "Oh, alright. Come with me."

Turning to his left he led the way through a side exit and into a narrow passageway that ran parallel to the kitchen. Halting midway he opened an unmarked office door and gestured for us to enter.

"I can give you a few minutes only. Make this quick."

Since Rohan had been deferential and soft-spoken when he offered to serve dinner after the tragedy on Saturday, I was surprised at this antagonistic reception. *He must channel his inner Gordon Ramsey while on duty.*

The room was claustrophobic with barely enough space for three adults to stand in. He pointed to two plastic chairs, offering us a seat, but he remained by the door, standing. He seemed keen to end this fast. *We should have invited him to join us elsewhere in the hotel after the lunch rush was over.*

"We're sorry to drag you away from your duties like this but Mr. Peiris asked us to gather some information. We just want to know what you remember from the events of Saturday night," said Vino starting off.

"Again?" he demanded. "I went through all this with the police! And I can't twiddle my thumbs here I need to oversee the kitchen. It's a disaster waiting to happen!"

"Yes, we understand," I said, as apologetically as I could. "But Mr. Peiris asked us to also speak to everyone, just to ensure nothing is left out. He wants this wrapped up as soon as possible."

Rohan let out a harsh breath and messed his hair. "Okay. There's nothing much to remember. We prepared all the food and waited and waited for service to begin. When it didn't, I went outside to find out what was wrong. I was told someone had been killed. I offered to serve dinner anyway until the police arrived."

"We were also wanting to speak to two of your helpers, Hasitha and Saman, about their stint at the bar on Saturday. Isn't it unusual that they are both on leave today?"

"They asked for some time off. I said okay," he snapped. "Are you telling me how to run my kitchen?"

"Of course not." I paused. "It's just unusual that you gave two workers the day off knowing there's a full house. Anyway, what we wanted to ask them was this. That night, at the bar, someone slipped a note for Serena under a drink. Since you were also helping at the bar, did you see anything?"

"A note?"

"Yes. Probably looked like the slips of paper used for the clues in the Mystery Game."

"Look here, Miss…"

"Kiyama."

"Kiyama" His voice was dripping with sarcasm. "I was at the bar for a short time and only because everything was ready in the kitchen. I admit I was curious to see how the game was progressing. Is that a crime? Should I have stayed 'below stairs'?"

"No. I'm not implying…"

He opened the door. "Please, go back to whatever marble hall you came from. I've wasted enough time talking about that stupid girl's death."

His behaviour put me on edge. Everyone else we had spoken to in the last few days had shown some sympathy for Serena, and a willingness to help. But not him.

"Did you know Serena?" I blurted out.

He blinked rapidly and clenched his fists by his side. "I have already answered these questions to the police!"

Rohan was breathing hard. His eyes flicked uneasily between us. Sweat stood on his forehead. With a sudden movement he spun around, slammed the door and clicked the lock. As he turned, he drew a knife out of the front pocket of his black apron.

I sat transfixed. I could see Vino's horrified face out of the corner of my eye. I dared not move a muscle.

He tightened his grip on the carving knife and waved it before our faces.

"I saw the police arrest those two guests earlier today. How did you two figure out it was me?"

"We didn't," I whispered. "We were just following the mysterious note…"

"You should have left that well alone!" he hissed.

I wondered how thick the walls of the room were. *If we goaded him into raising his voice, would someone outside hear us before he butchered us?*

"Since we are here, at least tell us why you killed her," said

Vino softly. "It was a near perfect crime."

I crossed my fingers and hoped that the compliments would calm him down and loosen his tongue.

Incongruously, it worked!

"Serena Perera," he said with disdain, "was a spoilt brainless *brat* who was set to inherit our father's vast fortune." Seeing our disbelief, he chuckled. "Yes. Perera is a common enough name, so I kept it. My mother was his 'piece on the side.' Oh, he sent a cheque now and then to ensure we didn't live in abject poverty. My mother was able to stint on luxuries and give me a good education and I left for the Middle East as soon as I completed my studies here. I did whatever it took, I worked as a bartender, among many menial jobs, until I was able to rise in the ranks. When tourism started to flourish here, I returned and worked at a few top restaurants. But my *father* refused to see me. Refused to give me the capital I needed to start my own place. I had the talent, but talent only gets you so far!

"I kept an eye on his businesses. I saw how my idiot of a sister was given a top job just because she was *a member of the family*. I watched from the side as she slept around, partied, and appeared in the gossip columns. Imagine my surprise last Friday when I realized she was a guest here, at this very hotel. I couldn't believe my good fortune!"

I bit my tongue. I had so many questions but asking them would stop the flow of free information. I glanced at Vino. She was fiddling with the sling bag by her side.

"It was *my* idea that some of the kitchen staff assist at the bar. *I* mixed most of Serena's drinks so that she got a good dose of alcohol into her system. I was afraid that she may have been too drunk to follow the instructions in the note, but it worked like a charm. The gods were on my side. No one interrupted us when I met her outside in the garden. In fact, that drug dealer and his shenanigans provided the perfect suspect to the crime. Later, I ensured that Hasitha and Saman didn't turn up to work in case they had seen something. Everything was going according to the plan… That is, until you two came snooping around!"

My mind was in a whirl as the pieces fell into place. Minosha had insisted that Serena usually held her liquor. If only we had considered that before: but it was too late now.

"But how can you be sure that even now, you will inherit her fortune?" Vino asked.

"He will *have* to acknowledge me now!" Rohan snapped, stepping forward. "I'm the last one standing!"

Suddenly, he laughed uncontrollably. "You all came here to play a murder mystery game. But I won in the game of life!"

Somehow, we had to survive this nightmare. A desperate plan formed in my mind. "If you kill us here, they will know you were responsible. Dozens of people saw us walk in here with you. Why don't you just leave us and go. Get away while you can. The police are otherwise occupied with the drug scandal. And like you said, it's the larger game of life. You can live, unfettered, if you go now. At the end of the day, it's just our word against yours. They have no solid proof that you killed Serena. You can still inherit your father's money if you play it smart. All you need do is wait for the furore to die down. But if you're caught…"

Something scratched at the door making us all jump.

Could that be a cat? Or a mouse? We've been playing a game of cat and mouse!

I struggled to control my panic-stricken thoughts and almost held my breath, waiting for him to decide.

The minutes mount to hours… All we have to decide is what to do with the time that is given us…

"You," he ordered finally, pointing at Vino. "Get up!"

Her legs almost collapsed under her as she struggled out of her chair.

"Reach over to that filing cabinet and open the second drawer."

She did as she was told. "What am I searching for?"

"There are some large serviettes stored there."

My heartbeat calmed a fraction, and I felt a surge of hope.

"Use them to tie you friend's hands and legs and gag her."

I nodded encouragingly at Vino. This was a good thing. Hopefully, he would leave us trussed up like turkeys and try to run. When she was done, he commanded her to toss the serviettes over to him.

"Place your chair opposite hers, sit down and put your hands behind your back."

"You've got to be joking!" she objected. "This place is so cramped we can barely sit abreast!"

Rohan tightened his grip on his knife. "Just do it," I hissed. *This was not the time to be picky!*

Once he was done, he returned the weapon to his apron pocket. "I hope you don't mind missing a few meals," he sneered as he unlocked the door, "it may be a few hours before anyone thinks to search for you in here. By that time hopefully, I'll be gone."

And stepped out… into the waiting arms of Inspector de Silva.

CHAPTER TWELVE

TWO HOURS LATER we had given our statements, gobbled a quick lunch, and adjourned to the rooftop which was the only place large enough to accommodate everyone involved. I was almost dancing with impatience to know how the police timed their entrance with such dramatic flair. Rohan's arrest was quick and painless for all parties involved and we were unbound as soon as possible. However, the good Inspector refused to divulge his secrets immediately and insisted that we wait for his return.

The news spread like wildfire that the Head Chef had been taken into custody for the murder of Serena Perera. Speculation was rife as to why he had committed the crime and I was certain Vino and I were the only people to know the entire story. Taking a leaf from the Inspector's book, we informed everyone that we preferred not to repeat the details and would wait for all to gather.

So it was that while all the luggage was stored in the lobby ready to be checked out, the participants of the ill-fated Saturday night game waited restlessly to find closure. It was teatime when Inspector de Silva finally graced us with his presence. The excited chatter of the waiting crowd died down as we all faced him expectantly.

"Thank you all for your patience. As you know, Mr. Rohan Perera, the Head Chef of this establishment was arrested this afternoon for the murder of Serena Perera and the abduction of Vinodhini and Kiyama. I must admit at the outset that the assistance of these two ladies led to his capture. We do not usually reveal the facts of an investigation to all and sundry but taking into consideration the inconvenience caused to all of you here, and how closely you were associated with the events of the weekend, I have decided to share a very concise version of what happened.

"I have spoken to Rohan briefly and what it boils down to is this: Serena was his half-sister. When he realized she was a guest for the weekend he took the opportunity to do away with her in the hope of being the sole beneficiary of their father's wealth."

Feeling like a schoolgirl I raised a hand. "I'm dying here. How did you know where to find us and how did you happen to be just outside the door?"

Inspector de Silva smiled. "Ah, the benefits of modern technology. You should ask your friend that question."

I stared at Vino. "What's he talking about?"

She grinned mischievously and said, "I downloaded a personal safety app onto my phone after our last fiasco and near brush with death and programmed the Inspector's number. We were lucky Rohan liked to talk so much – it gave me the opportunity to slip my hand into my bag and send the SOS alert!"

I must have looked as flabbergasted as I felt because everyone laughed. Minosha, Kumudu, Megan, Rob, and the Malwattes gathered around us, all talking excitedly and congratulating us on our investigative skills.

I waved them all down and turned to Inspector de Silva. "What about Chris and Chamil? They haven't returned to the hotel yet."

"Ah yes. Those two. I was on my way back to the hotel anyway when I received Vinodhini's SOS. It turned out that Chris could not have strangled Serena. He wears a carved ring that has tightened on his finger and cannot be removed. There was no corresponding mark on the victim's neck. We are holding them on drug dealing charges, but as the ganja did not actually pass hands and there was only intent to buy, he will probably walk with the help of a good lawyer."

Mr. Peiris moved to the centre of the room and clapped his hands to get our attention.

"Thank you, Inspector de Silva, Kiyama and Vinodhini for the wonderful work. We can all move on with our lives now! I have ordered tea and coffee be served here. Please enjoy a cup before you go back down. I believe everyone is checking out today. All the paperwork is complete, and you can leave as soon as you are ready."

The crowd broke up. Some heading for the refreshments while others gathered in smaller circles to discuss the case and say their goodbyes.

Seeing Megan and Rob holding hands I approached them in glee. "Hey there! I sincerely hope this experience has not marred your holiday. What's next on the agenda?"

"We've been set back by just one day. Thank you for solving the case so fast or else it would have truly messed up our itinerary. Our next stop is the cultural triangle. There's a car picking us up in…" Rob broke off as he checked the time. "It must be here already! We've got to dash!"

Megan squeezed my hand and whispered before leaving, "Please thank Vino as well. Rob was unexpectedly romantic, and I just couldn't stay mad at him for long." She winked. "He proposed all over again, with the ring hidden in a delicious chocolate cupcake! I doubt he came up with it by himself!"

I laughed and waved as they left. That, at least, was a happy ending. Seeing Riaz and Hamzah I smiled and started towards them next. But she glared at me and dragged Riaz off towards the exit. I was flummoxed. *What had set that off?*

Feeling a soft touch on my shoulder I turned to find Tracy Malwatte behind me, her eyes on the leaving couple. "Don't take it to heart," she advised. "I spoke to them at lunch today. Hamzah, unfortunately, believes Chris's allegations. And she disapproves."

My jaw dropped. So much had happened since the showdown in the lobby that I had completely forgotten the incident. "But I'm not…" I started, but she cut me off. "How you live your life is none of our business and not ours to judge," she said firmly. "I wanted to congratulate you on a job well done, my dear. If you are ever in Colombo please look us up. Now, excuse me, I need to extract my husband!"

I watched, still somewhat stunned, as she deftly steered Mr. Malwatte towards the exit.

The crowd had thinned out now. Catching sight of Minosha and Kumudu finishing their tea, I joined them.

"I'm sorry I couldn't speak to you before this," I said. "How are you holding up?"

Minosha looked upset. "You were right about having to field a lot of phone calls. All Serena's friends and family have been inquiring after what happened. My phone battery couldn't take it anymore!" she sighed. "Her parents are arriving today. They may already be here. I dread the thought of facing them!"

"You don't have to speak to them alone. Inspector de Silva will hang around a little longer if you ask him to. He probably knows they're due to arrive, anyway. And Mr. Peiris will also be here to explain things. You don't have to shoulder that burden alone." Changing tack, I asked, "Did you find the missing pendant?"

Minosha shook her head. "No."

I glanced at Kumudu, who shrugged.

"We'd better go down," she said as she dragged Minosha to her feet. "Oh, and thank you for your concern."

Another abrupt departure. I sighed and longed to get back home. This must be the longest weekend ever!

Soon only Mr. Peiris, Lavanya, Vino and I were left on the rooftop. The hotelier thanked us profusely once again and smiled when we reminded him of our deal.

"Of course! You're welcome to use our pool and spa facilities! Anytime!"

With that, they too were gone.

I sank back into a couch and allowed the silence to envelop me. The breeze had picked up. Birds chattered in the nearby trees. I swung my legs up and stretched out on the couch for a moment.

"Don't fall asleep now," murmured Vino who was curled up in an armchair opposite.

"Hmm..." I answered. "I feel emotionally and physically drained."

"Did you speak to Megan and Rob?"

"Yes! He took your advice and proposed again. Very romantic, was what she said."

"I know. She thanked me as well. I'm happy for them."

I opened my eyes and asked, "Did you speak to Riaz and Hamzah?"

Vino snorted. "He looked apologetic, but she ran from me! Oh well, you can't win them all."

"The Malwattes invited us over the next time we visit Colombo. I like them. We should keep in touch."

"Yes," she agreed. "And for the sake of my uncle as well."

"There's still one mystery left unsolved," I said. "What happened to Serena's pendant?"

Vino shrugged. "We can leave that one for the hotel management to deal with."

I sighed. "That's it then… Time to go home…"

Our quiet chat was interrupted by one of the waiters who handed me a sealed envelope. "This was left at the lobby for you, Miss."

I raised an eyebrow and tore it open. Inside was a single sheet of paper. It read:

KUMUDU HAS THE STOLEN JEWELLERY

I frowned and passed it to Vino. *What?*

She crumpled it and tossed it into a nearby ashtray. "Someone is playing mind games. I suppose we could hand this over to the police and check for fingerprints, but what's the point? They've all left by now. Do you think it's true?"

I nodded slowly, thinking it through. "Yes, it's possible. Minosha did say she was bitter about the boyfriend. Maybe Kumudu decided to even things out by taking the pendant?"

"And then left a note for us, in the third person…?"

"Or Minosha figured it out but didn't get the chance to speak to us privately. Maybe she's afraid to tell anyone what she knows?"

Vino dusted her hands. "Either way, it's not our problem anymore." She pulled me to my feet. "Let's go home."

The lobby was empty. The numerous bags of the other guests had been collected. Siril wheeled our luggage to my car as I handed our key to the reception desk and prepared to leave.

"Kiyama?"

I froze.

I knew that voice.

I turned towards the man who had been seated in a sofa facing away.

"Andy?!"

ABOUT THE AUTHOR

Nadishka Aloysius is a teacher, actor, and author. As a teacher of Drama and English Language with over twenty years' experience, and a mother of two sons who love story time, she finds inspiration in the little everyday details of life. Nadishka loves reading crime fiction and fantasy and this is reflected in her writing for Tween, YA, and adult audiences. She conducts creative writing workshops and school visits to share her love of literature. As an actor she prefers to play the antagonist since it allows her to explore the darker side of human nature.

The picture book *Roo The Little Red Tuk Tuk* was a Finalist at the Wishing Shelf Book Award. Her debut novel for children *Ronan's Dinosaur* was nominated for the State Literary Awards in 2019, while her first YA novella *Raavana's Daughter* was longlisted for the prestigious Gratiaen Award in 2019 and nominated for the State Literary Award in 2020. *That Easter Sunday* won the State Literary Award for Best Children's Literature Category II in 2021.

If you liked this book, please leave a REVIEW on social media or Amazon to encourage others to try it as well!

Other books by this author:

For Pre-Schoolers
Toran and the Alphabet Fairy
Roo, the Little Red Tuk Tuk
Eyesha and the Great Elephant Gathering
The Little Lost Fishing Cat
Dressing Up with Archchi

For Middle Grade readers
Ronan's Dinosaur
That Easter Sunday
Travel Journal for Kids

For Teenagers
Raavana's Daughter

For Adults
The Body in the Paddy Field
Murder at the Wedding
Death at the Fete (Only on Amazon Kindle)
Corpses in Colombo (Only on Amazon Kindle)

Find Nadishka Aloysius Books on    

THE BODY IN THE PADDY FIELD

Kiyama Fernando, an English teacher from Colombo, is fleeing a failed marriage. She visits her good friend Vinodhini Dias in a small town far away from her troubles. But, little does she know that trouble is about to come knocking soon enough... When the body of a local teacher is found abandoned in a paddy field and her friend becomes the prime suspect in his murder Kiyama concludes that the only way to help her friend, is to solve the murder before the police. As their investigation leads them from a paddy field to a rubber plantation, a gambling den, and a school, the two friends realise nothing is as it seems.

Will they uncover the killer before Vinodhini is taken away in handcuffs? Can they decipher friend from foe? Will the secrets they unearth lead them to an early grave?

ACKNOWLEDGEMENTS

This book would not be possible without the contribution of many people.

My heartfelt thanks go out to my family for their support; especially to my husband Rajeev for his invaluable feedback and to my two sons for giving me the space to disappear into the world of Parkaduwa.

A book is incomplete without the dedication of editors and beta readers; therefore, thank you Dinushka Fernando, Devika Brandon, Medhya Samarasinghe, and Lilamani Ebell – this book is what it is because of your input. I also must make special mention of my critique partners on Storyorigin Courtney Flagg and Ashleigh Stevens whose input was invaluable when crafting the story. And a big thank you to Evan Gow for creating a wonderful platform for the use of indie authors such as myself.

I would also like to thank all those who read the first book *The Body in the Paddy Field* – your enthusiasm prompted me to extend the series!

RAAVANA'S DAUGHTER...

Mermaids, Demons, Gods...It is 8000 years B.C. Sita Devi, the wife of Lord Rama, the Prince of Ayodhya, has been abducted by the Demon King Raavana. Hanuman, the Ape hero, is tasked with building a bridge to facilitate the invasion of Lanka. The Ape army gathers on the Southern coast of India. The expedition is however brought to a halt by the workings of the Mer-People who inhabit the Indian Ocean.

Follow Hanuman as he struggles to overcome their enchantments and complete his task. However, who is the mysterious Mer-Queen who lures him into her undersea lair? What part has she to play in this epic war? Is all fair in love and war?

The Ramayana is a Hindu Epic as old and as famous as Homer's Odyssey. However, it is not as well retold in Western Literature. This is a retelling of the Ramakien (the Thai version of the Hindu tale). If you are a lover of **Mythology, Historical Fiction, World Religions or Fantasy** - then this is for YOU!

Includes Places to Visit in Sri Lanka, linked to the Myth

CHAPTER SIX

Hanuman was appalled to see Mermaids active in the ocean around the island. There was no record of them inhabiting the waters of South India, and no seamen had reported a sighting - which, of course, did not mean they did not exist. Quickly, Hanuman formulated a plan. He was on his own. He needed to gather intelligence about the creatures in order to deal with the problem. Then he would have to uncover some magic or a talisman that would dispel the Mermaids. To do that, he would have to follow them into the water.

Hanuman had many powers. As a child he had acquired many boons from gods. Unfortunately, since he had used his new-found powers for mischief a great sage had cursed him, erasing all remembrance of them. When he was commanded to assist Lord Rama the curse was lifted. One power had already served him well in this war - the ability to fly. Another, yet unused, was the ability to survive underwater for a length of time. It was on this that he pinned his hopes as he dove into the water.

He swam with powerful strokes towards the shimmering light which improved visibility under water and turned the seabed into a floodlit garden.

The floor was carpeted in multi-coloured corals. Fish of all sizes darted in and out, seemingly undisturbed by the activity around them. Hanuman was careful to stay away from the razor sharp edges of the coral reef as he made his way towards the bridge. The bridge was a wonder to behold, floating above him like one of the King's roads that meandered through the countryside. It was broad enough for four horse drawn carts travelling abreast. He took a circuitous route towards the mermaids, who were too preoccupied with the destruction to notice his arrival. Hiding behind a large rocky outcrop, Hanuman observed more closely these fantastic creatures of the deep.

They were playful and terrible to watch. They were childlike as if joyfully breaking down a toy they had built themselves. They tossed the boulders between them in a game of catch. Hanuman noticed subtle differences in their size and shape, and realised that both male and female of the species were present. Some of the larger Mer-People used their strong tails to swat aside rocks and it soon became clear they were competing to see who could throw one the farthest.

Hanuman scanned the assembled crowd trying to decipher a command structure. Who was in charge of the mayhem? He noticed a group floating by the side of the bridge. The Mer-People formed a circle around a Mermaid who was more magnificent than the others. Her strong features were not as severe and her form was lithe. She was bedecked in pearls polished until they reflected the light. Her tail shimmered as if she wore cloth of gold interwoven with precious jewels. A crown of coral was on her lustrous hair, which streamed around her like a cloak. In her hand she grasped a trident.

He had found the Mer-Queen.